Blind Faith

The Abigail Baker
Mystery Series Prequel

By Mary B. Barbee

This is a work of fiction. All of the characters, organizations, and events portrayed in this novel are either products of the author's imagination or are used fictitiously.

Editing Team: Jenny Raith and Molly Misko

Cover design by Daniela Colleo of www.stunningbookcovers.com/

www.marybbarbee.com

Chapter 1

The night seems darker than normal, Faye's thoughts drowned out the sound of the car blinker as it clicked one last time and their car turned onto Sapphire Lane.

"It's really cloudy tonight," she said to her husband, turning her head to look out her passenger window then shifting in her seat and craning her neck to see out the back window.

Jim grunted in agreement, but Faye thought he seemed uninterested.

"Do you think the power is out?" Faye asked. "Oh wait, no, I see the Lang's lights are working." As they passed their neighbors' extravagant home, Faye could see the familiar spotlights light up the horse statue in the center of the Langs's large front lawn. Their lantern-style porch lights situated on either side of their driveway entrance glowed in the dark.

"Umhmm," Jim grunted again. The clicking sound resounded as Jim pushed the car blinker on again to prepare for turning into their driveway. Faye sighed. Jim was ignoring her, and she was instantly frustrated. The advice from their marriage counselor popped into her head: *Be present. Be patient. And you, too, will find peace.* Faye took a deep breath, but the reminder was short-lived and quickly faded back out of her thoughts.

"There's no one on the road, Jim. Why do you feel the need to turn your blinker on to turn in the driveway?" She asked with a mixture of insult and sarcasm, her southern drawl adding an extra unnecessary syllable to the word driveway. She continued without catching a breath, "And I swear, you've gotta be the slowest driver in Billingsley. It shouldn't have taken this long to get home."

Faye stuffed her cell phone into the side pocket of her purse and reached down to the floorboard to grab her favorite bright pink high heel shoes. She slipped her shoes on her bare feet, one by one.

Jim didn't respond. He continued to slowly pull the car into the driveway, straightening the wheel and taking his time shifting into park. Before turning the ignition off, he turned to his wife and said, "I think the real question here is why does my use of the car's blinker bother you so much?" His voice was flat and unemotional. He stared at his wife with a blank expression, waiting for an answer.

Faye rolled her eyes. "Fahget it," she said. She decided she didn't want to fight after all, especially after the nice dinner that they had together. Pointless and unresolved arguing had become typical for the couple. They simply couldn't make it an entire night without getting on each other's nerves in one way or another.

Faye fumbled with the door handle, carelessly hooking one of her polished acrylic fingernails on a small crack in the curve of the metal. Yanking her hand back, she cracked the false tip, and a sharp pain instantly shot into her nail bed. She let out a yelp.

Jim didn't react. He opened his car door slowly and deliberately like he did everything else. Stretching his long legs, he stood tall at six foot three inches. He turned to shut the door behind him carefully.

Forgetting again about how she didn't want to fight, Faye snapped, "I'm fine, Jim." She stepped out of the car, dramatically stomping her feet onto the driveway, her purse clutched in one hand. She slammed the car door shut. "Not that you care," she snapped again.

Jim remained quiet but waited patiently for his wife to walk around the front of the car and join him next to the sidewalk. The headlights of the car turned off automatically just as Faye approached, and the couple was instantly enrobed in darkness. Jim grabbed Faye's wrist gently.

"Wait," he muttered. "Why are our porch lights off?"

Faye felt the hair on her arms stand on end. She leaned into Jim's arm instinctively.

"I don't know," she spoke in a low voice as if someone might overhear her. "Maybe we forgot to leave them on?" Faye asked, knowing full well that forgetting to do something like that was completely out of character for Jim. They had been married for over twenty-one years, and Faye could not recall an instance that Jim had forgotten to turn the lights on before they left the house in the evening.

Jim shook his head as if he were trying to push away any suspicion and moved his hand down to grasp Faye's hand, interlocking his fingers with hers. He stood taller and began leading the way along the sidewalk to the front door in front of Faye. No longer whispering, Jim muttered, "No, something must be wrong with the power." Then, after a quick pause, he glanced back at Faye and said, "Weird that you were just saying that."

"Yeah, but then we saw the lights were on at the Langs's," Faye said in a hushed exasperated voice, gently pushing his shoulder as if to tell him to continue walking.

As much as Faye could get frustrated with Jim, she counted on him, and instinctively leaned in when he stepped up to take charge. Faye's thoughts drifted as she recalled several situations over the years when Jim acted as her rock.

When they were much younger and newly married, Faye remembered receiving the news that she was barren and wouldn't be able to have children naturally. She was heartbroken and could still feel the tightness in her chest as they sat together across the large mahogany desk in her doctor's office. She didn't leave the house for weeks. She couldn't control her emotions and she feared breaking down into tears in the middle of the grocery store or during one of her yoga sessions. Jim had taken a few days off work to comfort and care for Faye, but eventually he had continued his life, leaving her for work every day. That is when he began keeping a fresh bouquet of flowers on the small table by her bed, replacing the flowers whenever they started to droop. Faye loved waking up to the beauty and fragrance of vibrant fresh flowers, and she appreciated how Jim continued that gesture over the years, never missing a day - even though he always wanted credit for it in their arguments.

Another time, a few years later, they traveled to Europe together to celebrate their tenth anniversary, and Faye's luggage was lost during the plane trip. Jim stepped up and spent hours on the phone as Faye rested in a hot bubble bath, recovering from jet lag and trusting that Jim would solve the problem. Sure enough, Faye's suitcases were promptly delivered to their hotel room later that evening in time to get dressed for dinner. She could remember everything about the wonderful dinner, the elegantly set table, soft sultry music, and the delicious handmade pasta. But, Faye felt a familiar pit in her stomach as her thoughts turned to how small and unattractive she felt when Jim winked flirtatiously at the young beautiful waitress.

Faye's jolt down memory lane was interrupted by a cold wind that ripped through her thin dress sending shivers down her spine. "Wait, Jim," Faye said in a loud whisper. "Slow down. I can hardly see the sidewalk, and I'm wearing heels, you know."

Jim stopped and Faye released his hand to grab onto his shoulder instead. "For Pete's sake, we have lived here for fifteen years. I believe I could manage my way to the door on this sidewalk with a blindfold on," Jim said, finally showing irritation.

Faye remained unusually silent. She chose not to respond to Jim's snarky comment, and together, the two of them moved slowly to the front porch. They took the three porch steps in unison slowly, and Faye heard the keys jingle faintly as Jim pulled them out of his pocket to unlock the door.

He had a small flashlight on his keyring that provided enough light to see the keyhole. As he unlocked the door, Faye leaned in closer to her husband. Despite Jim's efforts to assure her things were fine, she couldn't shake the uneasy feeling that had first settled upon her the moment they turned onto their street. Jim pushed the door open and reached in to flip on the lights. Faye heard the light switch, but the interior of their house looked like a dark hole. She blinked to try and adjust her eyes to the darkness.

"Well, I figured. Something is up with the power," Jim said. "I'm gonna need to go down to the basement to check out the breaker box," he said from the front hallway. Faye felt Jim's hand brush her leg, searching for her hand. She grabbed tight as he gently guided her into the dark house. She noticed that the house still felt warmer than outside, in spite of the absence of light and power and thought that it must not have been out for long.

Faye stifled a yawn. "Ugh," she grumbled, "I just wanted to come home and go to bed. Why would our power be out when the Langs's seems to be working just fine?" She knew it was a rhetorical question, but her nervousness was mixed with annoyance and she was making no effort to hide her frustration.

"Well, I guess that's the golden question," Jim said, shining his small flashlight down the hallway towards the basement door, in a somewhat failed attempt to illuminate the way. "And that's why I have to go check it out. Let's shut the door, though. It's cold outside," he said, gently guiding Faye further into the foyer. He reached beside her and shut the door, turning the deadbolt. The small weak light from Jim's keyring flashlight bounced off the floor and walls like a pale ping pong ball.

"You're going to need the bigger flashlight. It's in the kitchen," Faye said, removing her high heels and setting them carefully on the bottom step of the stairs in front of her. "Let's go get it, and then I'll sit and wait for you in there while you deal with the breaker box." Jim was shining the light directly under Faye's face, and she pushed his hand away directing the light toward the kitchen. She nudged him to start walking, holding on tightly to his shoulder. She felt around with her free hand, reaching for the skinny table by the door as they passed, setting her purse down carefully, as she did each time she entered her home.

Jim began to shuffle down the hallway toward the kitchen slowly, one hand outstretched in front of him. Suddenly, Jim stopped dead in his tracks. Faye bumped into him slightly and overreacted with a loud, exaggerated sigh.

"What the..." Faye began. Jim spun around and briskly covered Faye's mouth with his free hand before she could finish her sentence. He held the flashlight up to illuminate his face and formed his mouth into a tight circle, lips puckered, as if to shush her. Faye's eyes grew big and she squeezed Jim's arm. It didn't take any special telekinetic energy to figure out that something alarmed him. Jim slowly removed his hand from Faye's mouth and switched the light on his small flashlight to off. Faye held her breath and listened closely, but the silence was as thick as the darkness. Her heart started racing, and Faye swallowed hard in an effort to fight back tears.

Faye felt Jim's hand cup the back of her head, his face leaning in close so that they were cheek to cheek. She felt his breath as he whispered into her left ear. Faye could barely make out what her husband was saying, but she heard, "I think someone is here. We need to go back out the front door as quietly as we can." Faye nodded, but before she could even move an inch, a bright light appeared from the kitchen, engulfing the couple in its rays. Faye felt paralyzed. She opened her mouth, but no sound escaped.

"Are you looking for this?" a loud deep voice came from behind the light. Jim turned to face the culprit behind the light and planted his feet firmly, pushing Faye behind him and placing himself between the intruder and his wife. He moved swiftly as if it were all one choreographed motion, once again taking charge.

"What is it that you want?" Jim commanded, his voice strong and steady. Faye wanted to run, but her bare feet might as well have been glued to the floor. Her knees were weak, and she leaned into Jim's back, resting her head between his shoulder blades, holding on tight to his shirt at his waist. Her body was trembling, and tears were rushing silently from her eyes.

The intruder remained silent and didn't answer, holding the flashlight still as a statue.

Jim repeated the question. "What do you want?" He asked again. His words fell out, a bit more foreboding the second time around.

Faye could hear and feel the fear in her husband's voice, yet somehow, it gave her the strength she needed. Her knees straightened, and her paralysis subsided. She turned and quickly walked a few steps back towards the front door, crouching down slightly, hoping to hide from the light. She reached the door and the moment her hand touched the deadbolt lock, she heard a series of sounds that would be rooted in her mind for the remainder of her life. First, Faye heard the deafening sound of a gun firing. Immediately after, she heard Jim cry out in surprise and finally, she heard what she intrinsically knew to be the sound of Jim's body hitting the wall and sliding down to the wood floor.

Faye screamed out and dropped to her knees. Her hands instinctively covered her mouth. Tears streamed down her face and her body trembled. She tried desperately to become invisible. The chemical smell that clung in the air instantly reminded Faye of the smell that lingered after fireworks. The light was still shining down the hallway, and she noticed it hit the wall directly next to her. She was hidden in the dark, but it would only take one quick flick of the wrist for the intruder to shift the flashlight and find her crouched in fear. She could see Jim laying on the floor, his hand on his chest, covered in dark red blood. He laid there, silent. Faye strained her eyes, trying to see if her husband was still breathing, watching closely for any kind of movement.

Remembering her own danger, she quickly slid over to the bottom of the stairs, leaning back to be sure she would remain outside of the path of the light. The darkness that unnerved her just minutes before now provided her a sense of safety. Faye huddled there for a few moments, her body trembling uncontrollably, as she heard the steps of the intruder slowly approach Jim.

Another bullet was fired, this time at close range. Faye's body stiffened, and she bit her tongue hard, stifling a scream. She quietly and quickly crawled into the adjacent living room and slipped into a small narrow space between the couch and the wall. She could no longer see Jim, but she faced the front door and considered if she would be quick enough to run, unlock the door and escape unharmed. She didn't have the courage, and she decided she would stay hidden for as long as she could. She focused on keeping her breathing steady but quiet.

The house was silent for only a few moments, but to Faye, it felt like an eternity. The circle of light on the wall at the end of the hallway, next to the front door, grew larger as the shooter walked steadily towards the foyer. The intruder's footsteps sounded like thunder, breaking through the silence step by step. Suddenly, the stream of light swung across the living room walls. Faye looked directly above her and could see the reflection of the light's glare on the picture frames hung on the wall above the couch. She held her breath and pulled her knees up closer to her chin, squeezing her shins as tight as she could.

Without another sound, the intruder turned his attention toward the front door. He was leaving! Faye watched from behind the couch as the shadowed figure reached for the deadbolt with the hand that held the flashlight. Turning the lock, the beam of light flashed up towards the ceiling, briefly illuminating the side of the shooter's face as he pulled the door open.

Faye covered her mouth and swallowed a gasp. Faye instinctively squeezed her eyes shut right at that moment, terrified to see this horrible person's face. The door shut quietly behind the intruder.

Sitting in the dark, tears rolled down Faye's face. After a long minute, Faye summoned the courage to crawl out of her hiding place, and with knees knocking, she made her way to the front door. With an unsteady hand, she locked the deadbolt and turned to feel in the dark for the table beside the door. Finding her phone tucked away in her purse, she dialed 911 and using the light of her phone, she made her way towards Jim's lifeless body.

The emergency operator answered the phone, and between sobs, Faye began to tell the 911 operator everything.

Jim was shot.

Yes, she was safe. The intruder left.

Yes, Faye saw the shooter's face, but for only a second. The only thing she could remember seeing clearly was that the killer was wearing a broad-brimmed hat.

"Yes, like the hats the Amish wear," she said, now annoyed with the questions. "Can you just send help?" she snapped at the 911 operator.

Chapter 2

Anna pulled the curtains open and smiled, gentle creases appearing at the corners of her mouth. She stood in awe as she watched snowflakes of all sizes drifted silently to the ground covering everything in sight in a magnificent blanket that twinkled and shined under the bright sun.

"Don't you just love a white winter?" Anna asked her twin sister, settling down on the couch sideways. Her knees were pulled close to her chest. Her feet were warm in thick navy blue socks, but she reached down to cover them with the folds of her plain dress. "I could just sit by the window all day."

"Mmhmm," Beth responded quietly. She was wiping the kitchen table with a wet dishcloth.

Anna turned her head away from the view of the winter wonderland and watched her twin sister methodically moving, thoroughly cleaning one section of the table before moving on to the next. Beth could become consumed with worry for what seemed to Anna like the smallest reasons sometimes, and most of the time, Anna knew what was on her sister's mind. This time was no different, but she asked anyway.

"Everything okay this morning, *Schwester*?"

"*Jah*, everything is fine," Beth said, her voice somber and melancholy.

Anna wasn't going to push it. She knew that Beth was fighting emotions, facing some big changes with her daughter moving to a new town just after the holidays. She also knew that Beth would talk when she was ready.

Beth rinsed and folded the washcloth, hanging it on the faucet before joining Anna on the couch in front of the window. The women looked like mirror reflections, facing each other, heads turned slightly. The identical twins sat together gazing out at the winter wonderland in silence.

"It is beautiful," Beth said quietly after a few minutes. Anna smiled, hoping that her sister's mood might have shifted even a little bit.

"*Jah*. We should enjoy these moments of peace because you know how chaotic and busy things get around here during the holidays," she said.

"True," Beth said, returning her sister's smile. "But you know I love all of it... the smell of pine from the Christmas tree mixed with the aroma of cookies baking in the oven. The sounds of our grandchildren giggling with excitement about beautifully wrapped presents. The happiness that just lingers in the air, and the big smiles on everyone's faces."

Anna nodded and reached over, lightly patting Beth's leg. "I know. Me too! And this year is going to be even more fun with Rosemary's first Christmas. It seems like it wasn't that long ago when we were young mothers ourselves. And look at us now with sixteen grandkids between the two of us!" Anna was so proud of her new grandbaby, Rosemary. The sweet little girl would be her oldest daughter's last baby, and she simply just couldn't spend enough time with her.

Anna noticed a tear slide down Beth's face as if it were moving in slow motion. She gasped and set her feet on the floor, reaching over to wrap her arms around her twin sister.

"I'm so sorry, Beth! I didn't mean to upset you!" Anna said, her words spoken through tears of her own.

Throughout their lives, it was inevitable that when one of the sisters cried, the other was soon to follow.

Beth rested her head on Anna's shoulder. "No, it's fine, *Schwester*. It's nothing you said really. I'm just struggling with having to soon say goodbye to Abigail and Jeremiah and the kids. It feels more and more daunting as each day passes and the moving date approaches.

"I never wanted any of my kids to move away. I imagined we'd all stay together in Little Valley forever," Beth said. She lifted her head and reached into the pocket of her apron, pulling out a white handkerchief with a beautiful pink peony embroidered in the left corner. As she wiped her tears, she continued pouring her heart out to Anna.

"I know I shouldn't be so upset. I should be happy for them. They are so excited to start their new life, and Jeremiah has such a great opportunity there with the leather-smithing shop. I mean, I *am* happy for them…" Her words trailed off as she wrung the handkerchief between her hands in her lap.

Beth lifted her face and looked at Anna, tears brimming over and said, "I really am. I am happy for them. I'm just going to miss Abigail so much."

Anna's heart ached with sympathy. She wanted badly to take away Beth's pain. She pulled her close again and hugged her tight, letting Beth cry onto her shoulder for a few minutes without conversation. Then, she gently pulled away and placed her hands firmly on Beth's shoulders.

"Okay. This is going to be hard. There's no doubt about that, *Schwester*. It's always going to be okay to cry and be sad about saying goodbye. She is your oldest daughter, after all! Of course, your heart is going to suffer a bit, but remember when we were little and *Maem* went on that long trip to Great Aunt's funeral? We were sick with a stomach bug at the time and had to stay home with Mrs. Swarey. Remember how we cried and cried when we said goodbye?"

Beth nodded, her tears had slowed, and her eyes locked with her sister's.

"And we talked late into the night about our fears that *Maem* might not ever come back?" Anna continued.

Beth nodded again and responded. "We prayed," she said.

Anna smiled. "That's right. We prayed." She paused. "We prayed because that is what *Maem* taught us to do when we're scared. So, we prayed late into that night, and we prayed every day that she was gone whenever we became worried."

Beth said, "*Jah*, I remember that."

"But that's not all. I know you have been praying, *Schwester*. I have been praying for you - and Abigail, too, of course. But the most important part of that story is that she came back. *Maem* came back safe and sound."

Anna held Beth's hand in both of hers and leaned in close. Her voice was quiet but serious as she said, "Beth, you must trust that Abigail will be safe and sound. You must trust that she will come back to visit often. This is simply a new chapter for her and her family. And it will be a new chapter for you. But it won't be the last chapter of the book. I promise."

Beth nodded. She wiped her face, took a deep breath, and then leaned forward and hugged her sister tight. "Oh, Anna, I know you're right. Thank you so much for always knowing what to say."

She pulled back, stuffed her handkerchief back into her pocket and held her sister's hands in her own. "That memory means so much to me," she said, "and I love you so much for reminding me of it. I love you, *Schwester*. I can always rely on you, *and* I couldn't be happier to have you right beside me as the main character in every chapter of my book!" She chuckled.

Anna grinned, "Well, we do have quite the adventure stories, don't we?"

Beth nodded, a wide smile set on her face. "*Jah*, I think it's safe to say we could definitely be characters in one of those mystery series we read."

The sisters laughed together, but they both knew it was true. As they changed the subject and rose to their feet to move forward with their day, a slight sense of apprehension remained in the air.

Chapter 3

Abigail stood and tucked a loose curl back under her *kapp*. She reached her arms toward the ceiling and stretched, arching her back and letting out a long breath.

"For sure and certain, packing is no fun," she said to her mother, grabbing a roll of tape off her dining room table and cringing at the screeching sound it made as she pulled on the end.

Beth nodded. "*Jah*, I agree. I guess you never know how much stuff you have until you have to put it all in boxes."

Beth reached for the marker and wrote *Living Room* across the top of the box, drawing a small heart over the letter *i* instead of just a dot.

Abigail pushed the box towards the others, lined up neatly against the wall next to the front door.

"I'm so excited for our trip out to Billingsley tomorrow," Beth said, hoping that her voice hid the sadness she felt about Abigail leaving.

"Oh, me too," Abigail responded, her face brightened. "I can't wait for you to see the town and where we're going to live and everything! I'm sure you and Aunt Anna could use a weekend away, too."

She grabbed her clipboard and began updating her list of things to pack before turning her attention back to her mother.

"Maybe we should take a break, *Maem*," Abigail suggested. "I can fix some tea and pull together some cheese and crackers. What do you think? Are you hungry?"

Beth nodded, "*Jah*, that sounds good. I'll start the tea, though. You can prepare the snacks."

Beth's knee let out a complaining crack as she rose to her feet. "It's not so easy getting off the floor anymore. I guess your *maem* is getting old, *dochder*," she chuckled.

"Ah, you're far from old, *Maem*." Abigail threw her arm around her mother's shoulders and squeezed tight.

"You and Aunt Anna are in excellent shape. I don't know anyone else who can solve crimes and catch the bad guys like the two of you." Abigail said. She winked and flashed a wide grin, exposing her naturally straight white teeth.

Both women laughed together, and Beth laid her head on Abigail's shoulder. They paused for a moment as Beth raised her head and turned toward her, comfortable in the silence. The mother and daughter stood just inches from each other, their profiles matching.

"Oh, Abigail, what am I going to do without you?" Beth said before quickly turning away, rubbing her eyes.

Beth didn't want Abigail to see her get upset again. She wished desperately that she could somehow stop the constant tears from forming at all. She reminded herself that this move was the best thing for Abigail, and it would be selfish of her to ask Abigail, Jeremiah and the kids to stay in Little Valley. And besides, like Anna said, Abigail would be fine. Safe and sound.

Abigail had made her way into the kitchen and as she pulled a box of crackers out of the cupboard, she said "Oh, you'll be just fine, *Maem*. We're only a couple hours away on the Amish taxi, and you have everyone else here.

"It just feels hard now, but I promise it's going to get easier," Abigail said in a comforting motherly fashion.

Beth nodded and wiped a tear that had escaped despite her efforts to keep it away. She headed toward the sink to fill the teapot with fresh water.

"Of course. I know, I know. I'm being silly." Beth said, her voice lighthearted. She waved her hand in the air as if she were shooing a fly.

"Let's not focus on the bad things anymore. Besides,'Gotte is there to give us strength for every hill we have to climb.'"

"Oh *Maem*, you have a proverb for everything," Abigail laughed as she set a block of cheese, a cheese knife, and a cutting board on the table next to a sleeve of crackers.

"Let's talk about the trip," she said, her hand pushing down on the knife. "So, it's going to take us about 2 hours to get there on the taxi..."

Beth wrinkled her nose. She much preferred her own driving to riding on the taxi, but she knew that it would take way too long to get there if they took her buggy, even with her new horse, Charlie.

The Amish taxi was simply a van that was driven by an *Englischer* to help Amish citizens travel to neighboring towns or sometimes further. Beth had ridden on the taxi only a couple of times her whole life. Once, she and Anna had traveled to Worthton to visit her cousin, and another time, she and Noah had taken a longer trip for his great uncle's funeral. Both times, she was cramped and felt a bit claustrophobic. She remembered wishing she could roll down a window but each time, neither she nor her traveling partner had secured window seats.

"Did you find out if Angel could ride on the taxi?" Beth asked. Angel was Abigail's golden retriever. She was laid out on her dog bed, positioned perfectly on the living room floor in a ray of sunshine streaming from the front windows. She lifted one ear as Beth mentioned her name.

"*Jah*, they agreed to let her come along for the ride," Abigail said. "Jeremiah was very pleased to hear that. He worries about us women traveling alone," she chuckled, "but I don't think Angel is much of a guard dog."

"We'll be fine, of course," Beth said, "but I'm glad that she's coming along, all the same. I think just having a larger dog in your company sometimes is a sense of security."

Angel stood and leaned into a downward dog yoga position, stretching her body, before mastering a body shake that started with her head and cascaded all the way down to her tail. Beth cringed as she watched the golden fur float into the air. She loved Angel, but the thought of having a house full of dog hair was enough of a deterrent for Beth to ever want a dog of her own. Noah had recently been wanting to adopt a dog. He peppered Beth at almost every dinner with facts about dogs that were "clean and hypo-allergenic." Beth didn't believe any of that for a second and stood firm on her concerns of the upkeep required.

Angel sauntered over to see what food Abigail was preparing and laid down again at Abigail's feet.

"Good girl, Angel," Abigail said. "You're excited to go on a trip with me and Grandma and Aunt Anna tomorrow, aren't you?"

"*Ach du lieva*, you act like she's a *bopplin*," Beth chuckled as she dropped tea bags into two small porcelain cups. "I think you often forget she's a dog."

She stepped over Angel and set the dainty little tea set down on the table. The set was handed down to Abigail, as she was Beth's oldest daughter. Abigail's great grandmother - Beth and Anna's grandmother - had first purchased it from an antique shop in the big city years before. Beth remembered how Abigail had always adored the set as a young girl, so when Abigail and Jeremiah were married, Beth and Anna knew just what to give her.

"*Denki, Maem*," Abigail said, ignoring her comment about Angel.

Beth sat across from Abigail and reached for a cracker and a slice of cheese. "So, *dochder*, I know you're excited about the move, but do you have any concerns at all?" Beth realized she was so caught up in her own feelings that she hadn't really considered how nervous Abigail might be about relocating to a new town.

Abigail slumped back in her chair. Beth thought she looked just like she did when she was a teenager.

"Not really," Abigail answered automatically, her eyes squinted slightly as if she were thinking. "Well, I mean, I guess there's the normal stuff. Like, we don't really know anyone there yet. I hope the kids can make friends quickly and that we fit in with the community like we do here. Plus, I want to make sure that I can find somewhere to sell my crochet, of course. I prefer selling my crafts in an established shop rather than having a table at a farmers' market, you know."

Beth nodded. Abigail did seem to have a lot of concerns after all. Beth was relieved that they would have a chance to visit Billingsley together this weekend. She decided to shift her focus and try to help resolve some of this for her daughter.

"Have you had any time to crochet lately, with the kids and the move?" Beth asked, after taking mental notes of all the things Abigail had just mentioned.

"*Jah*, I often have some time in the evenings after the kids are asleep. Keeping my hands busy helps clear my mind and settle any nerves from when I overthink things.

"I'm playing around with the thought of shifting from the shawls and scarves I've been making to these really cute little animals instead. Let me show you," Abigail said, as she stood and made her way to the sewing basket nestled next to the couch. Opening the basket, she pulled out a little bumble bee, a small frog holding a flower, and two colorful turtles, setting them out on display on the table in front of her mother.

Beth grinned and examined each carefully. "These are perfect, *dochder*! How cute!"

Abigail looked relieved to have her mother's approval. "Oh, good. I'm so glad you like them! They're really fun to make. You know how I love to finish a project, and these smaller projects are so easy to start and quick to finish.

"The only thing I haven't figured out yet, is how to add the leather knitting tags that Jeremiah makes for me," she continued. "After the move, when things aren't so busy, I'll work with him to see what we can make work."

"I know you'll figure something out," Beth said. "You've always been so creative."

"Well, I'm sure I get that honestly, *Maem*," Abigail smiled. "And I definitely got my attention to detail from you." Abigail laughed and reached over to touch her mother's arm.

Beth smiled back. "Why do I feel like I should apologize for that?" She giggled.

"Oh, no way," Abigail said. "I wouldn't trade that for anything in the world."

Beth placed her hand over her heart as if to say thank you, her eyes sparkling. The mother and daughter sipped their tea simultaneously.

"Overall, though, to get back to your question, I would say I'm more excited than nervous about moving to Billingsley," Abigail said. "It feels almost like a really exciting adventure.

"The town is beautiful, and everyone seems very friendly. I'm sad to leave you and my siblings behind, but I'm also looking forward to my new life. And honestly, it will be nice to escape constant reminders of all the crime that has been happening in Little Valley over the last year."

Beth winced. "I'm confident that the crimes are behind us now, but yes, I know what you mean. Thankfully, Billingsley does seem like a quiet and peaceful town. It is a huge relief knowing that you're moving somewhere safe and crime free." Again, Beth hoped the tone of her voice was convincing and hid her true fears.

As Beth cleared the table, Abigail began reading out loud all the things on her list that still needed to be done in the next few weeks in preparation for the move. Beth didn't hear a word she was saying. Instead, she recited a silent prayer while she carefully washed and dried the fragile teacups.

Gotte, please keep Abigail and Jeremiah and the kids safe in their new town. Stay by their side as they settle into their new home. Beth grinned as Angel rubbed up against her leg and laid down on the floor next to her. *Oh! and Angel, too, Lord. I almost forgot Angel.*

Chapter 4

Anna, Beth, and Abigail sat shoulder to shoulder on the back row of seats in the Amish taxi. Angel laid on the floor of the van by Abigail's feet. An Amish man and woman were the only other passengers, and they sat side by side in the front row, hastily boarding the taxi at the last minute, just before departure.

"Everybody ready to go?" the driver called out, looking in his rearview mirror. Abigail thought he seemed like a friendly trustworthy gentleman, at least that was her first impression. This came as a relief since she knew she would be relying on the Amish taxi to drive her from Billingsley back to Little Valley several times a year to see her family.

"*Jah*, we are all set back here," Anna confirmed.

"Yep, we're good to go," Abigail agreed. Abigail admired her aunt for her unending supply of confidence and courage. Her own mother, Beth, was initially uncomfortable around people she was just meeting, but Anna had a high enough comfort level for the both of them. It was determined years before Abigail was born that Beth was on the spectrum with high-functioning autism, and since Abigail was Beth's oldest daughter, she automatically tended to fall in line behind her Aunt Anna when it came to naturally wanting to protect her mother and help manage her stress.

"Okay, then, we're off to Billingsley!" the driver announced after getting confirmation from the couple in the front, as well. "We should arrive in just over two hours. Let me know if y'all get cold or need anything back there."

Abigail smiled at the driver's reflection and nodded. She reached down and patted Angel on the head. Angel's ear twitched slightly. She had already found the perfect position on the blanket that Abigail had brought for her and was drifting off to sleep.

"I'm so excited," Abigail said, her smile wide and eyes shining. "I was afraid we wouldn't be able to work out a girls' trip together before the move!"

Beth squeezed Abigail's hand and smiled. "*Jah*, this will be the first of many trips between the two towns, I think."

Anna was leaning forward in her seat, head turned toward Abigail and Beth, but her eyes were pushed up and to the left. She was listening, but not to Abigail and Beth's conversation.

"What's going on?" Abigail whispered, leaning forward.

Anna held one finger out in front of her, and then pushed her finger up against her lips.

Abigail eyes widened as she heard just three words, *he was murdered.*

"What are they saying?" she asked Anna.

Anna leaned in over Beth's lap and whispered to both of them, "I think someone was murdered in Billingsley."

Beth gasped and covered her mouth.

Abigail shook her head and whispered loudly, "No!" Her expression darkened as a mask of concern replaced her previous excitement. She craned her neck to hear more, but she couldn't make out anything over the sound of the heater that had just kicked on.

"Excuse me," Abigail called out. The driver looked in his rearview mirror and raised his eyebrows as if to ask if she needed anything. Abigail released the latch on her seatbelt so she could lean forward and tap the lady's shoulder, seated in front of her. The woman and man both shifted in their seats so that they could see the three women behind them.

Abigail leaned back and refastened her seatbelt. The driver realized Abigail wasn't trying to get his attention and returned his focus on the road in front of him.

"I'm so sorry to bother you," Abigail said. She was very aware that Beth was squeezing her hand tight, and she placed her free hand on top of Beth's in an effort to calm her nerves.

"I was just wondering if you all are from Billingsley?" Abigail knew she didn't recognize them from Little Valley.

The woman smiled a friendly smile and nodded. She said, "Yes. We are from Billingsley. We were just visiting our cousin in Little Valley. Maybe you know her? Mary Yoder?"

"Ah, yes, of course, we are very fond of Mary," Anna interjected. Then, after a brief pause, she made introductions. "I am Anna Miller, this is my sister, Beth Troyer, and Beth's oldest daughter, Abigail Baker."

"Oh! You are the one moving to Billingsley?" the woman asked with excitement.

"*Jah*, that's right. My family is moving there in just a few weeks," Abigail said, a bright smile on her face.

"It's so nice to meet you," the woman said, and the couple turned even more in their seats. "My name is Elise, and this is my husband, John Barkman." The man smiled, nodded, and touched the brim of his hat in a welcoming gesture.

"Oh, very nice to meet you two as well," Abigail smiled graciously. "My *maem* and Aunt Anna and I are headed to Billingsley for a short visit. I'm excited to show them your beautiful town."

Elise clasped her hands together, "Oh, that's *wonderbaar* news! We have been busy preparing for you. John actually helped the men build your new home."

"*Jah*, you will be very happy there," John spoke for the first time.

Elise continued, "I will let the ladies know you all are visiting. You must join us for dinner while you're here!'

"*Denki*," Abigail said. "That would be lovely! My husband and children and I are very excited for the move." The women continued to have lively conversation, sharing the names of their children, their husband's work and their hobbies. Beth's hand had relaxed, and she had started feeling comfortable contributing to the conversation as well.

Abigail had momentarily forgotten why she had originally tapped Elise on the shoulder, but when Elise shared some must-visit restaurants and must-see parts of Billingsley, something triggered her memory.

"Oh, that's right," Abigail said. "I had almost completely forgotten," she began, glancing at her mother. "Please forgive us, but did we hear you say there was some sort of accident that happened in town recently?"

"Oh, that was me," the driver interrupted. "I was telling the Barkman's here that Jim Roberts was killed in his home a couple nights ago."

Beth gasped and shook her head slowly as if she didn't want to believe it.

Abigail reached out and patted her mother's shoulder before responding. "I'm so sorry to hear that," she said out loud to no one in particular. Then, looking back at Elise and John, she asked "Did you know Mr. Roberts well?"

They both shook their heads and John said, "No. Well, we knew *of* him. He made it pretty clear that he didn't like us Amish folk, so I wouldn't exactly say we were friends."

Abigail's forehead wrinkled. "Oh," she responded. She knew it wasn't uncommon for there to be someone in the town that outwardly expressed their discontent toward the Amish communities. Little Valley certainly had their handful of citizens who felt this way and made it known to everyone, but she had hoped that Billingsley would be different. She was a bit disappointed to hear this.

Anna spoke up next. "That is just *baremlich*," she said. "The whole thing is just *baremlich*."

Beth nodded in agreement silently. Abigail glanced at her mother and thought she saw her eyes watering. She immediately wished that she had waited to ask Elise and John what happened.

"It's true that there are some circles of people in Billingsley who are not understanding of our lifestyle," Elise said.

John added, "*Jah*, and unfortunately, some of those circles have a bit of political power in our town."

"How do you mean?" Anna asked.

"Well, John just means that the mayor is not real friendly," Elise explained.

John interrupted his wife. "Jim Roberts was on the town council, and he was probably the most vocal person about his distrust."

"What about the police?" Beth asked. Abigail was surprised by the question, but she quickly put two and two together to figure out why Beth would ask that specifically.

Elise responded, "Oh, our chief of police is a woman, actually."

Anna and Beth exchanged surprised glances.

"*Jah*, she means business though, and she seems fair enough," John continued.

"Well, that's *gut*," said Beth. "I've never met a female chief of police, but I'm intrigued."

"And glad to hear she's fair," Abigail said, intentionally directing her comment her mother's way.

Soon enough, the conversation turned and continued instead with talk of all the wonderful things that Elise and John loved about their hometown of Billingsley. Becoming fast friends, Abigail was almost disappointed when the taxi pulled up in front of the Hi-Way Inn vacancy sign.

"We're here," Anna announced cheerily. Angel's ears twitched and she stood to her feet, giving her body a shake.

"Oh, no," Beth groaned. "We're going to be covered in fur now."

Abigail laughed, "Oh, poor Angel. Grandma gives you a hard time, huh?" She grabbed Angel's leash and stepped in front of her to lead her out of the van. She stepped down onto the paved parking lot and gently pulled Angel to follow her. She bent down so that her head was close to Angel's, scratching her under the chin. "You've been such a good girl! You had a good nap, huh?"

The driver helped Beth and Anna step out of the van one by one and then he turned to collect their bags from the back of the van. As the sisters thanked him, Abigail exchanged "see you soon" goodbyes with Elise and John before heading to the grass with Angel in tow.

The van drove away and Anna and Beth stood by their duffel bags, waiting for Abigail and Angel to join them. Angel was sniffing all around, and Abigail said quietly, "Go potty, Angel girl." Then she called out to Anna and

Beth, "We'll be right there!" and watched as her mother and her aunt twisted at the waist and reached for the sky, stretching in unison like two mirror images. As they stretched, the two sisters appeared to be engaged in a serious discussion. Although Abigail was out of earshot and couldn't hear what they were saying, she was pretty sure she knew the hot topic.

As she approached, the sisters ended their conversation.

"All ready now, Angel?" Anna asked, reaching down to pet the dog's head. Angel lifted her head as if to get a better scratch.

"She's good to go," Abigail said. "Shall we go check in so *Maem* can change into something not covered in fur?" Abigail's voice was lighthearted. She winked at her mom, linking her arm in hers.

"*Jah*, that would be *gut*," Beth said, chuckling.

"C'mon you two," Anna said. "I've got Angel. You carry the bags." She took Angel's leash from Abigail, turned, and headed for the office before anyone could object. Abigail carried two of the bags, checking the weight of each first to make sure Beth was carrying the lightest of the three.

A bell tied to the inside handle rang as the door opened, and the three women and Angel filed inside. A petite woman with blonde straight hair and a thin face was standing behind the desk, her eyes and nose red as if she had recently been crying.

"Hello, welcome to Hi-Way Inn," she said. Abigail thought her cheeriness sounded fake and forced, but she greeted her with a smile as if she didn't notice.

"Thank you," Abigail said. "It's good to be here."

"I suppose you are Mrs. Miller, Mrs. Troyer, and Mrs. Baker?" the woman asked, looking at her computer screen.

"Yes, that's right," Abigail confirmed. "And my dog, Angel, too. I called a few days ago and confirmed that pets are allowed?" Abigail politely posed the sentence as a question.

"Of course, yes, that's right. We do welcome most breeds of family pets. Angel is totally fine to stay here with us, thank you for checking." After Abigail, Beth and Anna signed the necessary paperwork, the woman turned to gather the room keys. "I have two rooms reserved for you. They are right next door to each other and share a door between them," she explained as she handed the keys to Abigail. "Please just lift the phone during regular business hours if you need anything at all. It will ring the front desk here, and I'll take care of you."

"Thank you very much," Abigail said.

Anna interjected. "What did you say your name was, Miss?" she asked with a warm smile.

"Ah, my apologies," the women's cheeks turned slightly pink. "My name is Elizabeth, but around here they call me Lizzie. My husband and I are the owners of the Hi-Way Inn. And you two ladies are clearly twins," she said, really looking at the ladies for the first time since they arrived. "My goodness, I've never met a pair of identical twins before."

Abigail chuckled, "Yes, my mom and my aunt are identical. I can tell them apart, but there is often a lot of confusion for someone meeting them for the first time." She grinned.

"Well, welcome again to Billingsley, ladies," Lizzie said, leaning forward on the counter, her mood had clearly lifted since they first arrived. "Is this your first time visiting?"

Anna responded. "Yes, it is. Although Abigail and her family will be moving here in just a few weeks."

"Oh, that's exciting!" Lizzie said, smiling big at Abigail. "Well, like I said, let me know if you need anything at all while you're here. I can recommend the best coffee shops and restaurants, and so forth. And this is a great location because you can walk almost anywhere from here. We're right smack dab in the middle of town."

"Thank you so much," Abigail said. "*Maem* and Aunt Anna, are you ready to go get settled?"

Beth nodded graciously at Abigail, and Anna said, "Yes, I think so."

"Do you want me to help you to your rooms?" Lizzie asked.

The hotel couldn't have more than ten rooms total, Abigail thought, but she glanced at Anna and Beth before answering, "I think we'll be fine, but thank you anyway," Abigail said politely. The women gathered their things, waved goodbye and made their way out the door, pulling Angel behind them.

The walk to their rooms was short as Abigail had suspected. They were quickly inside and getting settled, the twin sisters in one room and Abigail and Angel in the other. The door between the two rooms was open just slightly, and Abigail could barely hear Beth and Anna chatting in their neighboring room. Abigail went through the motions of unpacking and setting a water dish on the floor for Angel. As she was placing Angel's blanket on the floor for her bedding, her mind wandered back to the conversation in the taxi.

Surely, this isn't a bad sign, Abigail thought. She was sure that if Jeremiah knew about the murder, he wouldn't have let her come alone without him.

Chapter 5

Police Chief Amy Edwards stared out the window, her brow wrinkled. She was deep in thought, analyzing the few clues left behind at the scene of Jim Roberts' murder over and over again in her mind.

Any stranger walking in would take one look at Chief Adams's desk and think she was terribly unorganized. Papers appeared to be strewn randomly across the desk, cup rings formed years before she had even graduated from the academy peeking out at every corner.

The police station was set up at the end of Billingsley's oldest strip mall, sharing a wall with a barber's office and a few doors down from a used bookstore and a dry cleaner. It was a few minutes before seven and the early morning sun's rays were streaming through the clouds, creating long shadows across the nearly empty parking lot.

Chief Edwards made it a point to arrive at the station earlier than the others. She was a loner and took advantage of every moment of peace and quiet she could. This morning, she arrived even earlier than normal so that she could have some extra time to plan for the busy day that awaited her.

The sound of a car door pulled the chief out of her deep thoughts, and she stood to look out the window to see who had arrived. She wasn't surprised to see that it was Billingsley's newest and youngest police officer, Andrew Stokes. She rose from her desk and turned to add some coffee grounds to the coffeemaker.

"Good morning," Officer Stokes said in a sing-songy voice as he opened the door.

The chief stood with her back to him and rolled her eyes. "Morning," she mumbled.

The young man slid his arms out of his overcoat and hung it on the coat rack by the door. "How are you?" he asked sincerely.

Chief Edwards knew that Officer Stokes was a genuinely nice guy, but she felt like his positivity was a bit over the top. "Good," she responded, blowing the steam off her second cup of coffee.

She sat down and reached for a piece of paper, about the fourth one from the top of the pile, placing it on top, front and center. She leaned forward in her chair and rested her elbows on her desk. The title, Coroner's *Report,* was printed in bold letters at the top of the paper. All the important details were handwritten before the report was faxed over, requiring a bit of effort to read, but the chief had already deciphered it and practically memorized it. All the same, she searched again for something she may have missed.

Two gunshots in the chest, one appearing to be at close range. No other signs of trauma. Cause of death: homicide. The victim was forty-six years old and had been in good health. The bullets had been removed from his chest and sent to the lab for analysis. Chief Edwards expected to hear results early that morning, as well as any fingerprints collected from the scene.

The chief reached for the witness statement. It had been a home invasion. The killer was waiting in the Roberts's home when they arrived from a night out. According to Mrs. Roberts, the couple had a wonderful evening together and came home to a dark house. It was assumed that the intruder had flipped the breakers in the basement before they arrived. When Chief Edwards questioned Faye Roberts that night, she mentioned that the intruder had a flashlight, that Faye was trying to escape and run back out the front door when the intruder shot and killed her husband. Instead, she hid in fear, and the intruder left just minutes later.

Chief Edwards grabbed her bright pink pad of sticky notes and a pen. It had become a habit of hers over the years to write down her thoughts. She found it usually brought more clarity than trying to organize everything in her head.

Why did the killer leave Faye behind? she wrote quickly on one sticky note before pulling it off the pad and sticking it to the witness statement. Her thoughts continued: The killer knew Faye was still in the house when he left. Clearly, this was personal towards Jim, and for whatever reason, he didn't want to kill Faye. Chief Edwards was pretty sure that explained cutting the power. He expected to leave a witness behind, but he wanted to make sure he couldn't be identified.

Next, she wrote, *No robbery.* There was nothing missing from the house that Faye noticed yet. The killer definitely had one focused purpose, of that there was no doubt. She pulled the sticky note off the pad and stuck it next to the first.

Chief Edwards pondered on what could be the motive for killing Mr. Roberts. This is the piece of the puzzle that was missing, and she was going to have to do a bit of digging to uncover it.

Mr. Roberts had been a resident of Billingsley for his entire life, from what Chief Edwards understood. He had a lot of old friends who could potentially share some secrets with her, but she had a feeling she might learn more from those who wouldn't necessarily call themselves friends of his.

Chief Edwards scribbled *Amish hat* on the next sticky note, tore it off the pad and stuck it directly in the center of the witness statement. She knew that she would have to approach the Amish community and ask some questions, if only because of Faye's statement that the intruder was wearing a broad-brimmed hat "like the Amish," but the Chief had doubts about that lead. She had never had an ounce of trouble out of the Amish people in the town, and actually, quite the opposite. Everyone in their community seemed genuinely friendly and kind.

Chief Edwards was aware that Jim Roberts was quite vocal about his concerns at the town council meetings and had been actively proposing a bill to raise taxes on the Amish business income, and even their property, with the hopes of driving them out of town. The chief wasn't sure just how much support he had, however, and assumed it was harmless ranting that would eventually be replaced by something more important. Still, she would need much more convincing to consider someone Amish would feel threatened enough that they would seek revenge or take such drastic actions to put a stop to it.

Officer Stokes cleared his throat to get Chief Edwards's attention. She turned her head and raised her eyebrows.

"Can I help with the Roberts case, Chief?" he asked. His voice sounded a bit nervous and unconfident.

The chief paused and looked down at her notes. She knew a murder case was not common in Billingsley. She couldn't even be sure there had ever been a murder in town before, but she also knew that Andrew was eager to learn and advance in his career. She recognized that he arrived early every day, only second to her arrival. And he was the first to volunteer whenever she needed anything at all, whether it was to empty the trash in the kitchen, do some research on a case, or even go help old Mr. Finn out of his bathtub again.

"Sure," she answered, after a long pause. Officer Stokes looked like a little boy, just learning he was going to Disneyland. "Wanna ride with me today to poke around and see what else we can find out about why someone would want to kill Jim Roberts?"

Officer Stokes nodded so emphatically that the chief thought he might hurt his neck. She stifled a grin.

"Okay, so we're going to start with the neighbors. It's the Lang family, and I told them I'd come by this morning to ask a few more questions." Chief Edwards said, raising her cup of coffee to her lips. Taking a sip, she wrinkled her nose.

"First, though, we're going to grab a decent cup of coffee to go from Gladness and Joy," she said, referring to her favorite place to buy pastries, coffee, and sometimes lunch.

"Coffee's on me," the young officer said, eagerly. "Ready whenever you are... and thank you, Chief, for including me. I won't let you down."

Chief Edwards nodded and pulled her coat on, "Just take good notes, Officer Stokes." She approached the door with Officer Stokes right behind her just as Officer Kent Singer was entering. He was wearing a cowboy hat, as usual, which the chief always thought looked mismatched with his blue police uniform.

"Morning, ma'am," Officer Singer said. "You two headed out already?"

"Yes," Chief Edwards answered. "We are going to continue the investigation into the Roberts case. Can you make sure you stick around here and call me right away when you hear back from the lab? We're waiting on results of fingerprint testing as well as the type of gun used."

"Roger that," Officer Singer responded, mocking a salute off the brim of his cowboy hat. "You'll be the first to know when I get the call." Then, in a more serious demeanor, he said, "Be careful out there, though. It's crazy to think we have a murderer on the loose right now."

Chief Edwards nodded. "Always, Officer. I'm always careful, but thanks for the reminder. We'll be back in a little while. Call me right away if anything unusual happens while I'm gone."

They exchanged goodbyes and the chief and Officer Stokes headed out to her patrol car. The chief started the engine and the two sat quietly for a few moments as the car warmed up a bit. Chief Edwards noticed that the sun had risen higher in the blue sky and the shadows had disappeared. She couldn't help but think of the irony that with new light cast, darkness fades away, revealing what couldn't be seen clearly before. Her hand rested on the gear shift, but before putting the car into reverse, she wished silently for all the answers that she was searching for to come to light just as quickly as the sun rises in the sky each morning.

Billingsley was a safe place to live, and she planned to keep it that way.

Chapter 6

"*A*re you ready to go get some lunch, *dochder*?" Beth says, popping her head into Abigail's room.

"*Jah*, I'm starving," Abigail said, slipping her feet into her shoes and setting down her crochet. "Should we stop by the office and ask for a recommendation?"

"*Jah*, *gut* idea," Beth responded, tucking nonexistent stray strands of hair into her *kapp*.

"Okay, let's go," Anna said, and the three of them donned shawls, and Abigail slipped a red warm sweater on Angel, snapping it together under her belly. With Angel back on her leash, they headed out, locking their hotel room doors behind them.

They wandered back into the office, the bell clanging against the door for a second time that day. A man entered from the back room, surprising them, as they were expecting to see Lizzie. He had wavy brown hair and was tall with an athletic build. He seemed pleasant enough, in a heavy customer service sort of way. Abigail wasn't quite sure how authentic the friendliness was and felt a bit on edge. Angel growled quietly but stopped immediately when Abigail corrected her and tugged slightly on her leash. She glanced at her mom instinctively. She had never seen Angel act like that before and shrugged it off as maybe just new surroundings. This was, after all, Angel's first road trip.

"Welcome, ladies," the man said with an open grin, straight white teeth peeking out between his lips. "What can I do for you?" He is either ignoring Angel's behavior or he didn't notice it, Abigail thought to herself.

"Oh, hi," Anna said. "We were expecting Lizzie."

The man tilted his head back and said, "Oohh, right. Lizzie is running some errands. I'm her husband, Brody Wright. You ladies getting settled in okay?"

"Yes, thank you," Abigail responded. "We were actually just coming by because Lizzie offered recommendations for nearby restaurants. We're headed out to find a place to sit down and have some lunch."

Brody nodded, "Well, I'm sure you've heard of Gladness and Joy?" he asked. "The owners are Amish like you, which you probably coulda guessed by the name. And it's the most popular place to eat breakfast or lunch around here."

Abigail couldn't pick up if Brody had ill intent behind recommending an Amish place, but it sounded perfect to her. She glanced at her mother and aunt and they both nodded.

"Is it close enough to walk to?" Anna asked.

"Oh, absolutely. It's not far at all," Brody assured them. "Just head down this main highway and turn left at the first street. That's Main Street. It's about a tenth of a mile down, on the right. You can't miss it."

Abigail, Anna, and Beth thanked him and headed out the door. Brody wished them a *"gut* day," as they left. Abigail and Beth exchanged glances again.

"He was certainly peculiar," Beth said.

Abigail nodded, *"Jah,* I don't know what to think of him. Angel certainly didn't get a great first impression."

"I saw that," Beth said. "That was odd behavior for her."

Anna waved in the air as if her sister and niece were over-reacting, "I can't take you two anywhere. You're a couple of scaredy cats. Brody was odd, *jah,* but we have a handful of odd people back home in Little Valley, too, you must remember."

"You're right, *Schwester*," Beth said. "It sure is a beautiful day. I, for one, am grateful for the walk after that long ride."

Anna agreed and the two of them fell into conversation about how nice it was to meet Elise and John Barkman, the comfort of the van, the sights they saw along the way, and how they couldn't wait to tell Noah and Eli all about the Amish taxi ride.

Abigail trailed a bit behind the twin sisters, with Angel walking beside her. She was having a harder time shaking off the worrisome thoughts about the murder in Billingsley. She said a quiet prayer asking *Gotte* for the day's upcoming excursions to help her return to that excited feeling she had before the conversation in the taxi.

The three of them came across Main Street and turned left just as Brody had directed. Turning off the highway and onto Main Street felt like instantly stepping into a different town. Their view changed from the boring highway lined with dead grass and speckled with litter was replaced by a view that looked like a scene straight out of one of Abigail's favorite books. Abigail had visited Billingsley one time before with Jeremiah and the kids, but today, it seemed more lovely. Main Street was peppered with magnificent evergreen trees. The streetlights were shaped like lanterns, a festive lighted wreath hanging from each one. Pushed up perfectly against the edges of the sidewalk was thick green grass, and Angel immediately wanted to stop and explore.

"No way, Angel," Abigail said. "You are not going potty on that beautiful grass."

Beth and Anna paused, and both pointed at the same time. "There's Gladness and Joy," Beth said, excitedly.

"Oh, good," Abigail said. "Brody was right. That *was* an easy walk."

"It looks like there's a place right next to the building where Angel can go potty," Anna said. Sure enough, there was a sort of alley where the grass didn't seem quite as pristine.

"Perfect!" Abigail said. "I'll go ahead and take her over there and then find a place to tie her leash. You two mind going in and grabbing us a window seat so we can keep an eye on her?"

The sisters agreed, and the three of them crossed the street. Horses and buggies were parked outside of the restaurant right next to a couple of cars. Abigail's comfort level was quickly returning to normal. Angel did her business and Abigail fastened her to a post right at the front of the shop. She could see her mother and aunt settling into a booth on the other side of the glass. She patted Angel's head, pulled a rawhide-free bone from her pocket, and gave it to her. "That ought to keep you busy for a while," she said before heading in to join the sisters.

As she walked in, the lady behind the counter called out, "Welcome to Gladness and Joy!"

Abigail smiled warmly and responded, "*Denki*!"

There were three women wearing simple long dresses and *kapps*, preparing food and coffee drinks behind the counter. Another younger woman was serving those seated at tables. On the right side of the shop were shelves lined with goods of all kinds. She would be sure to remember this place, Abigail thought, as she quickly glanced at the baked goods, homemade jellies, jams, popcorn, and spices lining the shelves before making her way over to where Beth and Anna sat.

"This place is *wunderbaar*," Abigail said, as she squeezed into the booth next to her mother. Both Anna and Beth were looking down at their menus. Abigail leaned over to make sure she could see Angel from her seat, and then followed suit, picking up her menu and reviewing all the many selections. Her stomach growled quietly.

"*Jah*, did you see the *schtore*?" Beth said, without looking up.

"I did," Abigail said. "Everything looks delicious over there. But I didn't see your famous butterscotch cinnamon rolls," she smiled impishly.

"Not yet," Beth said, and they all giggled.

The waitress approached their table, greeted them, and set a mason jar filled with ice water in front of each of them. "Do you have any questions about the menu?" she asked politely.

Anna spoke first. "This all looks so *appeditlich*! It's so hard to choose." She smiled warmly.

"Oh, yes, I know what you mean," the waitress responded. "Is this your first time here?"

Anna nodded, and all three of them set their menus down on the table and shifted their full attention to the waitress.

"Well, I would recommend the butternut squash quiche, if you are looking for a brunch idea. It is made with fresh eggs and cheese - and it's very popular. If you want more of a lunch idea, we also have delicious panini sandwiches, and our soup of the day today is potato. All of our breads are made right here, and oh, whatever you decide, you must leave room for dessert. People just rave about our pecan pie and our coconut cake." The waitress paused and waited to take their orders.

Anna and Beth always ordered different things and then shared so they could taste both, so one ordered the quiche and the other ordered a turkey panini with cranberry sauce, cream cheese, and spinach. Abigail ordered a half club sandwich and a cup of the potato soup.

As the waitress collected their menus and walked off to turn in their order, Abigail asked the twins, "So, what do you think you might want to do after lunch?"

"I think after all this food, we should take a walk down Main Street," Beth said.

"Oh, I agree," Anna said, and Abigail nodded.

"I would like to help you find a shop while we're here that might be interested in selling your crochet," Beth said.

Abigail agreed.

"Where is the shop that Jeremiah will be working at located? Is it here on Main Street?" Anna asked.

"Oh, no," Abigail said. "The shop is a little bit more in the country where there are horse stables."

"Ah, that makes sense," Anna said.

The women sat and passed the time catching up on the latest with Abigail's children, Emma and Jo. Abigail told them how Emma had taken up an interest in painting somewhat sophisticated still life paintings with oil paints that Beth had gifted her for her tenth birthday.

"Jo is turning out to be quite different from his namesake, however," Abigail explained. Her youngest child and only son was named after her beloved brother, Jonah. Jonah and Abigail had a special bond that had developed as they were growing up together. Abigail was going to miss him terribly after the move.

Beth smiled, "*Jah*, he is not very much like his uncle."

Abigail rolled her eyes. "I know. Jonah is so adventurous and a free spirit. My little Jo is quiet, nervous, and would just stay in his room and read all day, if I let him."

"Well, reading books can be an adventure of its own," Beth said, defending her grandson. "He's such a kind child. That's not different from Jonah."

"That is true," Abigail said. "I worry about him the most with the move, honestly. I hope he can make friends quickly. Emma never has a problem fitting in, but Jo is much more reserved."

Anna piped in, "Kids are so resilient. And they change so quickly. He may be a totally different person in a year or two."

Beth nodded, "*Jah*, I remember when you were young and meek like that, Abigail. I feel like it was just a phase, though. By the time you hit your teenage years, you were so much more confident."

"*Jah,* it took your mom much longer than that," Anna winked at Beth.

Beth grinned, "I *still* get nervous. I wouldn't use the word confident to describe myself, for sure and certain."

"Ah, *Maem,* you are careful. And that can be just as important as being confident," Abigail said. "And besides, it balances the two of you. Aunt Anna has enough confidence for the both of you, but you, *Maem,* are the thinker. You question the important things, and that's never a bad thing."

Both sisters agreed, and Beth squeezed her daughter's hand.

Their conversation was interrupted by their food being served. One of the ladies behind the counter had brought it to them.

"I wanted to personally welcome you to Gladness and Joy," she said, as she set their lunches on the table in front of them. "My name is Sue Renno. My family owns the place. Where are you all from, may I ask?"

Anna spoke up, introduced everyone, and explained that Abigail was moving to Billingsley.

"Oh, I'm delighted to hear that! You all must come over for dinner this evening. We close the doors here at 4 pm, and we can have dinner ready by 6 pm, if that works for you," she said, her hands clasped in front of her.

"We would love that," Abigail said. "*Denki*!"

"*Wunderbaar*! Where are you staying? I will send someone to pick you up."

"We're at the Hi-Way Inn," Abigail said.

"That's perfect! It's not far at all," Sue explained. "Enjoy your lunch! I look forward to getting to know all of you more this evening."

Sue returned to her spot behind the counter, and silence fell over the table as Abigail, Anna, and Beth dove into their food.

"Everything is so *appeditlich*," they mumbled between bites. Each of the women had a taste of everything, humming in delight as they chewed. They vowed to return for breakfast the next day and approached the counter to thank everyone several times as they were leaving.

"Enjoy your time in Billingsley," Sue called out from the back, her hands wrist deep in a ball of dough. "We'll see you this evening!"

Anna, Beth, and Abigail left the restaurant with full bellies and smiles on their faces. Abigail collected Angel who was still working on the bone she had given her earlier. She pulled a folded reusable bag out of her pocket and slipped the now slimy bone inside. "You can finish it later, I promise," she told Angel as she untied her leash.

"Now, to walk Main Street," Anna said cheerily.

"*Jah*, let's go," said Beth. She linked one arm with her sister and the other with Abigail. "What a fun time we're having," she exclaimed.

Abigail smiled at her mother. She was so glad to see her happy. Abigail knew that her upcoming move out of Little Valley was going to be hard for her mother, and she had hoped that this visit would make things easier. So far, it looked as if everything was going as planned. Abigail exhaled a quiet sigh of relief and matched her steps with the twin sisters, who were already in sync.

Chapter 7

Angel barked excitedly, pulling at her leash and pushing off the ground with her front feet. They had just returned to the Hi-Way Inn after a couple hours of shopping on Main Street and had not yet reached their rooms.

"What is so exciting, girl?" Abigail asked, wrapping the leash around her palm a little bit tighter. She looked up to find a horse and buggy pulling into the parking lot. The horse was jet black just like her family's horse, Bella, and the buggy was identical to hers, as well. Sitting tall in the buggy, holding the reins, was a woman who also looked very similar to Abigail. She wore a simple gray dress, cream colored apron, and her dark hair was tucked neatly under her *kapp*.

Anna, Beth, and Abigail all stopped and waved hello, and she made her way towards them, parking the horse and buggy right outside of the room next to theirs.

"*Gute daag*!" she said, as she jumped down.

"*Gute daag*," the three responded almost in unison. Angel was quiet now, but still stretched forward, tail wagging and open mouth shaped like a smile, panting slightly.

"I'm Rose Swarey. I've come to pick you up for dinner," she said, excitement in her voice. She continued before anyone could respond. "I know, I know. I'm early, but when I heard you were in town, I was excited to see you, and I thought you might want to come see your new house, Abigail." Her words poured out like a racehorse running for the finish line. "I didn't know if I would catch you here or not. I figured you might be still shopping on Main, but thought I'd give it a try. And, well, here you are!"

The three of them stood there with smiles on their faces, waiting for Rose to take a breath.

"But, if you need time to *redd up*, that's totally fine. I can either wait for you out here, or I can come back, if you'd rather," she continued without pause. "I didn't think about the fact that you might want time to relax."

Finally, someone else had a chance to speak, and Anna said, "Well, *denki* for coming to pick us up, and it's a pleasure to meet you. I'm Anna Miller, this is my *schwester*, Beth Troyer, and her *dochder*, Abigail Baker."

Abigail and Angel stepped forward. "*Jah*, it's great to meet you, Rose. And this is Angel, who apparently really wants to meet you, too," she laughed.

"Ooohh, aren't you the cutest thing," Rose cooed as she bent down and petted Angel. Angel dropped and rolled onto her back. They all laughed.

"I guess she really likes you. She has given you permission to rub her belly," Abigail chuckled.

"Well, thank you very much, Miss Angel," Rose said in a sweet tone, leaning over to accommodate her. She looked up at Abigail and grinned. "Please tell me Angel is also moving to Billingsley?"

Abigail nodded, "*Jah*, she's coming with us, for sure and certain."

Anna interjected, "What do you ladies think? Want to quickly change our clothes and then head over to see Abigail's new house before dinner?"

"*Ach jah*," Beth said, "I can't wait to see your new home, *dochder*! I only need a couple minutes to get ready."

"Me too," said Abigail. "If you don't mind the wait, we can be ready very quickly."

"No problem," Rose said. "Take your time. If you'd like, Abigail, I can see if Angel here needs to go potty over in the grass there before we head out. The ride over is short, though, I promise."

"*Denki*, I'll be right back then," Abigail said, handing over Angel's leash. Angel was sitting at Rose's feet, tail still wagging when Abigail, Anna and Beth headed to their rooms to freshen up for their next adventure.

When they were ready to go, they locked up their rooms and all piled into Rose's buggy, heading toward the Amish community. Abigail sat next to Rose, with Angel squeezed in next to her, while Beth and Anna sat on the bench seat behind them.

"Did you grow up here?" Abigail asked.

"*Jah*, for the most part," Rose said. "We all came over from Ohio when I was a very little girl, so Billingsley feels like it has been my forever home. It's rare that we have new people come in, like yourself, so everyone is very excited." She turned and smiled at Abigail.

"*Vell*, we are certainly excited, too," Abigail said. "My husband, Jeremiah, and I grew up in Little Valley, and it's the only home we've known. We love it there and are happy that it's only a couple hours away by taxi."

"I think you're really brave for moving to a new town, but I know you're going to love it here," Rose said, pulling the reins slightly to the right to signal for the horse to walk closer to the edge of the road and let the car behind them pass.

Abigail heard her mother say to Anna, "She is a very good driver." She grinned to herself when she heard Anna respond, "*Jah*, she's a much safer driver than you, *Schwester*." Beth responded, but Abigail couldn't make out what she said. There's no doubt Beth's response was something quick and witty. Her aunt Anna always complained about her mother's driving, but Abigail knew that Anna secretly enjoyed having the freedom that came with Beth wanting to drive, and Abigail was also sure that if Anna didn't trust Beth's driving, she would not ride along with her.

Just as promised, the ride was short, and before they knew it, Rose was signaling her horse to turn onto a long unpaved road off the highway. Laid out in front of them several hundred yards away and slightly downhill as if hiding from the highway, was a cluster of houses and barns with farmland and open fields surrounding the community.

"Here we are," Rose sang out. As their buggy approached slowly, Anna, Beth and Abigail fell silent, taking in all of the sights. The landscape was beautiful with more evergreen trees stretching for the bright beautiful sky, not a cloud in sight. Women were taking laundry off clotheslines, folding and dropping them in baskets by their feet.

Women and men both were seen tending to their gardens. Children of all ages were running around, laughing and playing. Some dogs and cats were sleeping in their sunny spots on front porches, while others were roaming around, exploring, or playing with the children.

As they approached closer, people stopped to see who was coming. They smiled and waved as the buggy passed, calling out "*Wilkumme!*" Dogs barked friendly greetings, but Angel sat tall in her seat, quiet and regal. Chickens roamed, some even in the road, but moved out of the way of the horse as they passed through.

There was a sense of harmony, and Abigail instantly felt at home. She turned and glanced back at her mother, who smiled and nodded. Abigail knew she felt it, too.

The buggy turned one last time, pulling in next to a house on the far end of the community. It was painted white, like the others, with flowers blooming in the flower boxes attached to the windows, and there was a cozy little front porch equipped with a swing.

"*Wilkumme* to your new *haus*, Abigail," Rose said, as she set down the reins and hopped out of the buggy.

Abigail gasped and covered her mouth. She breathed the words, "It's perfect!" Angel jumped down, not waiting for Abigail, and made her way to the front porch, laying down as if to say she also thought her new home was perfect.

Abigail stepped out and helped Anna while Rose helped Beth out of the other side. Entering the home, they proceeded to explore the hardwood floors, the window over the kitchen sink that looked out over a backyard that looked like it had no boundaries, the exposed beams in the living room and kitchen areas, and the quaint simple bedrooms and bathroom.

"This is all really just *wunderbaar*," Beth said. "The only thing missing are some flowers planted in front of the house, but we can do that together next Spring."

Abigail nodded and reached out, squeezing her mother's hand. "*Jah*, I can really picture everyone here."

"You will still need a stable and small barn, though," Anna said. Abigail nodded.

"I think the men wanted to work with your husband to build that, Abigail," Rose said.

"Oh, he'll be happy to hear that," Abigail said.

After a few more minutes admiring the home, Beth and Abigail making mental notes about the cabinet space and discussing what furniture would fit best where, Rose asked, "Shall we head on over and meet the others, then? We can leave the buggy here for now, and I'll have Micah feed and care for the horse."

The group headed up the road on foot and stopped to meet each new face on the way.

"It will take me some time to remember everyone's names," Abigail repeated several times, met with extended grace from each community member.

In the center of the community sat a simple building that was built as a single room, its purpose for gatherings when the weather was not ideal for sitting outside. It blended in quite well. With its exterior resembling a house, Abigail hadn't even noticed the building as they passed earlier. The doors were propped open and there were tables and chairs set up inside in preparation for the night's dinner.

"Wow, this is *wunderbaar,*" Anna said. "We need something like this back at home." Beth agreed.

Beth turned to Rose, "How can we help?" she asked. Women were starting to show up with dishes wrapped in towels to keep them warm, and children could be heard responding to the enticing smell of delicious food, complaining of being hungry. Men were gathered in the side yard at a cluster of picnic tables, in what appeared to be friendly conversation.

Before Rose could answer, attention shifted to the road they had traveled on earlier. A police car was slowly making its way down the gentle slope into the community.

"Why are the police here?" Beth was the first to ask the obvious question.

Rose sighed. "I'm afraid they're probably here to ask about the death of Jim Roberts." She flashed an apologetic look at Abigail.

"We heard about that on the way in," Anna said. "Surely they don't think someone from the community could commit murder, do they?"

Rose shrugged. "Chief Edwards has always treated us with respect, but we've also never been through anything like this. Let's just pray that the real killer is found and everything is put behind us quickly."

Beth nodded, and she moved to stand between Abigail and Anna, holding their hands tight. All eyes watched as the police car parked in front of the community center. Chief Edwards and Officer Stokes stepped out of the car at the same time. Abigail's first impression of Chief Edwards was one of respect. She saw a woman, aged forty-something she would guess, her hair tied back in a bun, her athletic body dressed in a conservative police uniform, and a small, but warm smile, on her face.

Three older men with long beards stepped forward and greeted Chief Edwards by name.

"What can we do for you folk, today?"

"Well, I think we need to have a talk. I'm sure you've heard by now that Jim Roberts was murdered in his home on Thursday night," Chief Edwards said.

The men nodded and expressed their condolences.

"Well, I guess I just have a few questions to ask some of you. It's all protocol, you understand," the chief continued. Officer Stokes stood next to her, holding a small pad of paper and a pen.

"Yes, we've heard about it. And we also know that Mrs. Roberts is trying to pin the murder on us," one of the men piped in. Abigail sensed a bit of contempt in his voice, and she was sure the chief of police noticed it, too. It made her feel uneasy. She wanted to walk away, but for some reason couldn't.

Rose leaned over and whispered to Abigail, "Should we go inside?"

Abigail shook her head slowly and responded, keeping her eyes on the discussion that seemed to be escalating somewhat, based on the men's body language. "Maybe we should invite them to eat with us."

Rose grinned. "I like the way you think," she said.

The chief asked directly, "It is true that Mrs. Roberts stated that the killer was wearing an Amish hat, and to be honest, that is what brings us here tonight."

The men were silent and waited for the chief to continue.

"So, I guess I could ask where each of you were on Thursday night ..." Her voice trailed off as if posing a question.

The same man that spoke before interrupted, "*Jah*, you could indeed ask all of us where we were the night Mr. Roberts was murdered," he paused before continuing, "and we would all tell you that we were right here with our families, getting rest for the next day of work. None of us have any reason to be out on the town late into the evening."

Abigail watched as the other men wrinkled their brows. One man scoffed loud enough to be heard, and the other kicked the dirt at his feet.

The chief of police nodded without smiling. "Look, I'm on your side here. I don't know if I've made that clear. But when I'm told the killer was wearing a hat similar to the ones y'all wear everyday, you understand I have to question it."

The man who seemed to serve as the spokesperson for the group leaned in and said, "Ma'am, do you think if any of us were going to kill someone, we would have worn our hat to be identified?"

"Well, I guess that is a really good question, isn't it, Deacon?" The chief tilted her head and stood taller, placing her hands on her hips. She was studying the men closely.

After what felt like a long silence, the chief said "I think we have all we need here, then" She nodded to Officer Stokes. "We'll be back if we have any other questions, and you be sure to let us know if you hear anything else." She handed the deacon a business card.

Abigail watched as the men walked off, muttering under their breath, their faces flushed.

Rose grabbed Abigail's hand and pulled her toward the car as the chief and Officer Stokes were preparing to leave. Abigail heard Beth gasp quietly when she released Beth's hand and followed Rose.

"Chief Edwards!" Rose called out, waving her hand.

The chief turned to look in their direction, as did all the other eyes in the group. She shut the door and began walking toward Rose and Abigail.

"I wanted to introduce you to the newest member of our community, Abigail Baker," Rose said. "She and her family are moving here in just a few weeks."

Abigail felt her face fill with color, as she was not particularly used to this much attention, but she reached out her hand and invited a hand shake hoping she came across more confident than she felt.

"Well, it's nice to meet you Mrs. Baker," the chief said, shaking her hand. "Welcome to Billingsley. Where are you coming from?"

"Oh, not far," Abigail said. "I'm moving here from Little Valley, just a couple hours south of here."

"Oh, I know Little Valley," Chief Edwards said, with a grin. "That's a beautiful town, and I've heard a lot of great things about the Amish community down there." She glanced up and nodded at Beth and Anna, as if she knew they were also from out of town.

"That's my mother, Beth Troyer, and my aunt, Anna Miller. They're traveling with me this weekend," Abigail said, waving the sisters over. As they approached, Chief Edwards introduced herself and welcomed them to Billingsley as well.

Their friendly chatter was interrupted by commotion coming from the picnic tables where the men were gathered. Voices raised suddenly in anger between a few of the men were met quickly with hush demands. There was clearly some sort of disagreement among them, and none of it was missed by Chief Edwards. She watched the group with hawk-like eyes as the men tried to recover and then act as if nothing had happened.

"Should I go check on things, Chief?" the officer next to her asked.

The chief responded after a short pause, "No, that's not necessary," she said, her eyes still watching as the men fidgeted and then settled down.

"Would you like to join us for dinner?" Rose asked abruptly.

Chief Edwards returned her attention to the ladies and smiled, "That's very kind, but we should get going. We have a busy night ahead of us." She paused and then said, "I'll take a raincheck, though. I know it will be delicious."

Turning to Abigail, she said, "It was a pleasure meeting you, and I wish you a safe and easy move up here."

"It was a pleasure meeting you, as well, Chief Edwards," Abigail said politely, and the twin sisters agreed.

The chief began to walk away, but stopped and turned back abruptly. She pulled a business card out of the chest pocket of her uniform and extended it to Abigail. "Here's my number, if you need anything at all," she said. Her eyes looked as if she were saying more, but Abigail wasn't quite sure what.

Abigail took the card, and thanked her again. She slipped the card in her pocket and waved as the police car drove back up the hill towards the highway.

"Time to eat!" The dinner call couldn't have been better timing. Abigail, Beth, and Anna exchanged glances that assured Abigail that they were on the same page.

Rose pulled them into a small circle and said, "Now, just to give you a quick rundown, the guy that was murdered... he was on the town council and was trying to pass a ridiculous bill which would make our community pay more taxes than other citizens. And surprisingly enough, there are a handful of people in town who were actually supporting the bill. It's a long story, but his wife... she says that the killer was wearing an Amish hat."

Beth shook her head. "That's *baremlich*," she said. "Surely no one from this community is responsible for this," Beth posed her sentence as if it were a question.

Rose looked at Abigail with worry in her eyes before casting her eyes down. "*Vell,* we are praying for answers. That's all I really know."

Chapter 8

Abigail laid on her back in bed, staring at the ceiling and listened to Angel's steady breathing coming from her spot on the floor next to the bed. *She's sound asleep, no worries in the world*, Abigail thought.

Abigail's mind was racing, however. She had tossed and turned most of the night. She, Anna and Beth all had a wonderful time at dinner the evening before, and after Rose had driven them back to the inn, the three of them stayed up chatting a bit before turning in for the night. Their conversation was mostly replaying different conversations they had with different members of the community, comparing their favorite dishes, and reveling over Abigail's new house. But just as Anna said goodnight and retreated to the bathroom to get ready for bed, Beth came into Abigail's room and the mood changed quickly.

"I'm worried about what happened when the police arrived, *dochder*," Beth had said in hushed tones. "Did you see how the men reacted? I fear that there are some dangerous secrets being held there, and it makes me nervous. I worry about you and Jeremiah and the kids getting caught up in something..." Her words trailed off.

Abigail had expected Beth to be worried after all of that. It was normal for her mother to worry about things incessantly, especially when it came to her safety, but she hated that this was happening when the whole point of this trip was to set her mother's mind at ease. And if Abigail was being honest to herself, she would have to admit that she was also a bit worried.

Why would the men act so suspicious if they had nothing to do with the murder? Or were they just acting out of fear that they were actually being framed for a crime they had no hand in? Abigail had definitely seen firsthand how quickly their communities could be blamed for crimes they did not commit. That was one of the reasons she had come to peace with leaving Little Valley and moving to Billingsley. There were a handful of times just in the last year where crimes committed were either crimes against the Amish or someone from the Amish community was the prime suspect.

Rose's words kept playing over and over again in her head. The wife said the killer was wearing an Amish hat. *Why would she lie about that and try to frame someone?* Abigail turned over and laid on her stomach, propped up by her elbows, her hands clasped. She said a quiet prayer asking for *Gotte* to help Chief Edwards solve the crime quickly so that she and her family could move into a community that was peaceful and happy, and that her mother's worries would subside.

She sat up and stretched, vowing to clear her mind of worries and think only happy thoughts for her last full day in town. She opened the curtains and sat at the table by the window in her nightgown, crocheting and watching the sunrise over the tall trees until she heard movement in her mother and aunt's room next door.

A soft knock and the door pushed open, "*Ach du lieva*, you are already awake, dear?" Beth said, her voice sleepy.

"*Jah*, I have been up for a little while now. It must be all the excitement," Abigail grinned. "How did you sleep?"

"Very *gut*," Beth said. "Your aunt and I want to get ready and go back to Gladness and Joy for breakfast."

"*Jah*! Me too!" Abigail said. "I'll get dressed and take Angel out to wake her up. Give me about twenty minutes?"

"Perfect. We still have to say our morning prayers."

Angel stretched into a perfect downward dog position before doing a full body shake. Abigail poured dry dog food into her dish, and Angel's ears perked up a bit. She sauntered over as if she were in no hurry but quickly cleaned her plate and loudly gulped water from her bowl to wash it down.

While Angel ate, Abigail slipped into her navy-blue long dress and light blue apron, stepping into her shoes. She pinned her curly dark hair back and placed a clean white *kapp* on her head, tucking in stray strands. She wrapped her shawl around her shoulders, buttoning it in the front.

Turning toward the door, Abigail saw Angel standing in anticipation of her morning stroll. "Are you ready to go potty, sleepyhead?" Abigail asked, attaching the leash to Angel's collar, and petting her behind the ears. Angel watched intently as Abigail slipped the bag with yesterday's bone, along with a roll of poop bags, into her pocket and opened the door. Angel pulled her gently toward the end of the parking lot and then around behind the rooms where she found a perfect spot of soft grass on which to first sniff and then do her business.

"Good girl," Abigail said, leaning over and picking up the poop with a bag. They walked back around the front of the inn and reached the garbage can just as the twin sisters were locking their door. Abigail waved and called out, "*Gute mariye!*"

She jogged towards them, Angel keeping up with her stride right beside her, and greeted the ladies with hugs.

"One second," she said, "I just need to get my things, and we can go." She handed Angel's leash to Beth and headed back inside to grab a small bag of crocheted items, her billfold and room key off the table. Sitting there next to her key was Chief Edwards's business card. She went ahead and grabbed that, too, dropping everything into her empty pocket. She took one more quick glance in the mirror before heading out the door, locking it behind her. "Okay, I'm *redd up*," she told the sisters.

The sisters sat shoulder to shoulder in the same booth as the day before, with Abigail sitting across from them this time. Angel laid outside the window, happily gnawing on her bone. They each ordered a different flavor of *ebelskivers* to share and waited next for their coffee. The sisters chatted about how their *maem* had prepared similar stuffed pancake balls when they were young children, and how excited they were to see them on the menu.

"I'm excited to check out the gift store that the woman told us about last night. What was her name, do you remember? I've been trying to think of it all morning," Anna said.

"That was Helen," Abigail said. "*Jah*, how exciting would it be for them to buy my crochet?"

"Ah, Helen, *jah*," Anna said.

"Of course the store will want your items, Abigail. The work that you put into your crafts really shows in the unique details. Those little animals are so unique, too," Beth showered Abigail with compliments.

"*Vell*, it's so easy, since I enjoy doing it so much," Abigail said. "I don't expect to make a lot of money, but it would be nice to contribute a little bit to the family, if I can."

"And there's the benefit that 'Pride in your work puts joy in your day.' That's always been one of my favorite proverbs," Beth said.

Just then, Sue brought coffee to the table, first setting beautiful little porcelain mugs in front of each of them. She set a large coffee pot in the center of the table and placed a small glass bowl of creamers and a small wooden box filled with different types of packets of sugar.

"*Wie bischt*, ladies? Did you have a *wunderbaar* time last night?" Sue asked with a friendly smile.

"*Ach jah*," Abigail said. "We can't thank all of you enough for such generous hospitality."

Sue waved her hand in the air as if she were shooing a fly. "*Denki* is not necessary. You're a part of our community now, and we all had a wonderful time getting to know each of you. If everyone in Little Valley is just like you, then it must be a pretty *wunderbaar* place."

"That's very nice of you to say," Anna said.

Beth chimed in, "Little Valley is pretty special." Her face beamed as she talked about her home.

"Well, I just hate that the whole murder business came up while you were visiting, though. It was set to be a perfect night except for that," Sue said, shaking her head.

"Did you know Mr. Roberts?" Beth asked sincerely.

"*Ach jah*, everyone around him knew him. And, honestly, he had never been personally rude to me or anyone in here," Sue said.

"He visited Gladness and Joy, even though he wanted to raise taxes?" Abigail asked.

Sue nodded. "*Vell, jah*, Jim and Faye came here quite often. He was fond of our cinnamon rolls. I will say that Jim had more of a pleasant demeanor than his wife, for the most part. And they never seemed very happy together. They actually tended to bicker quite a bit, I noticed."

Beth stirred cream into her coffee. "That's interesting," she said aloud. "Have the police questioned you about any of it?"

Sue looked confused, "*Nae*, I'm not sure why they wo uld..." The intonation at the end of her sentence rose as if she were asking a question. "Do you think I should talk to the police about that?" Sue looked instantly worried.

"I think my sister may have read too many mysteries," Anna said with a chuckle. "I'm sure the police will find the person they're looking for before too long."

"*Vell*, we sure hope so," Sue said.

"I don't think it would hurt to share what you know with the police," Beth said. "You never know, they might find it helpful," Beth said, ignoring Anna's attempt to brush things under the rug.

Abigail interjected, "*Jah*, but you could just say something in passing next time Chief Edwards is in here. I'm sure she visits Gladness and Joy. This place is so good!"

"*Ach jah*, Chief Edwards comes in here a couple times a week. She was here just yesterday. And I think you're right. I will mention it to her next time I see her. That's a *gut* idea. *Denki!*"

Sue excused herself to get back to work, and Anna turned to Beth. "What are you doing?" she asked her sister, her tone held a hint of accusation but mixed with lightheartedness. "Are you trying to solve the murder?" She grinned.

Beth shrugged. "*Vell, nae*, not exactly. But it would be nice if the killer was caught before Abigail moved here, wouldn't it?"

Abigail reached out and touched her mother's hand. "*Maem*, you don't have to worry. I'll be fine."

Anna pleaded with her sister, "Now, let's enjoy our breakfast and talk about things that are not related to the murder, okay? I mean, we are headed home tomorrow. There's not even enough time for you to solve the case, Beth, so please leave it to the professionals this time."

Beth nodded, taking another sip from her coffee and looking out the window. After again savoring every single bite of their delicious breakfast, the three of them headed out for another walk through town. They traveled down Main Street and turned right onto Third Avenue. After passing a two-story house that had been renovated into a dress shop and a cute little storefront with a display of a wooden toy train set in the front window, they found themselves standing in front of Everything's a Gift. Strings of fairy lights lined the front window, lighting up a table decorated with handmade candles, beautifully painted greeting cards, dainty beaded necklaces and matching bracelets, and folded screen-printed t-shirts that had the town's name fading into a design of a colorful sunrise.

Abigail couldn't wait to walk inside and see what else lined their shelves. She quickly tied Angel's leash to the hitching post in front of the store, slipping the small piece of bone that was left in her pocket into Angel's mouth. As she pulled the door open, a gentle chime sounded, and she was met with a faint fragrance of vanilla.

"*Wilkumme* to Everything's a Gift," a friendly voice could be heard from behind the counter. A middle-aged woman with a round face, her gray hair tied loosely in a bun on the top of her head, smiled at Abigail, Beth, and Anna, as they entered.

"*Denki*," Abigail and Anna responded cheerfully and in unison. Beth waved and smiled, too.

"Are you visiting Billingsley?" the woman asked kindly.

Abigail nodded, "Yes," she answered in English, noticing that the woman was not wearing a *kapp*, "we are visiting from Little Valley, but I will be moving here with my husband and children in a few weeks."

The clerk clapped her hands in excitement, "Oh, that's exciting! I have visited Little Valley a few times myself. I just love the farmers' market there!"

Abigail smiled, "Well, you've probably seen my mother and my aunt before, then. They sell the most delicious baked goods at the market."

"Those sugar cookies?" The woman closed her eyes and placed her hand on her stomach. "There really is nothing like them in the world." She opened her eyes and smiled. "It's nice to meet you all. I'm LouAnn Ranch, but you can call me Lou."

"I'm Abigail Baker, and this is my mother Beth Troyer and my aunt Anna Miller. It's a pleasure to meet you."

Anna and Beth both nodded, smiled, and said "Pleasure" at the same time.

"Your shop is very nice," Anna said. "So many wonderful things!"

"Well, thank you," Lou said. "It's been my passion project for about 20 years now. Almost everything in here is made locally. Even though I'm off the beaten path of Main Street, I still manage to draw in customers, especially on the weekends and when it gets close to the holidays. Did y'all see my new sign on Main Street? My grandson made it for me, painted that red arrow on it, and the drugstore was nice enough to let me set it up on their corner. Everybody's pretty nice here, really... well, except we did just have that terrible crime happen. Y'all heard about that, I guess?"

The ladies nodded.

Lou waved it off. "Well, I'm sure Chief Edwards will figure that out soon enough. She's a great police officer, you know."

"Yes, we got to meet her last night, and we've heard she is very fair," Abigail said.

Anna spoke up, changing the subject. "Just looking around, I don't see any crocheted items. Do you have anything like that yet, Lou?"

"Well, no, I don't guess I do," Lou frowned.

Abigail smiled graciously at Anna and proceeded to show Lou the set of little turtles that she had crocheted a week before, and ask if she would be interested in adding them to her shelves. Lou said she just adored the handiwork and insisted that she would be honored to carry them. She proposed that they start off on consignment until word gets out and they start flying off the shelves, and she asked Abigail to bring in whatever she wanted whenever she was ready.

Abigail couldn't believe how easy that was, and thanked Lou, chatting with her a bit more as the sisters looked around and picked out a few gifts for their grandchildren. As Beth and Anna were paying for their items, Angel was barking, so Abigail headed outside to see what she was all worked up about. Exiting the shop, she found Angel on her feet, her body stretched long as she barked loudly at something across the street. Abigail didn't see anyone in sight, and she knelt down next to Angel, petting her on her head. Angel whimpered a bit and then went back to finishing her bone. Confused but relieved that Angel had stopped making a ruckus, Abigail stood up and brushed off her dress. Straightening up, she looked around, and there, directly across the street, she saw it.

It was a hat shop. Neutral colored straw hats and wool hats sat perched on a small hat rack right in the front window display. Abigail immediately recalled what Rose had said the night before.

...his wife... she says that the killer was wearing an Amish hat.

The sisters were saying goodbye to Lou, exiting with Lou directly behind them.

Abigail interrupted, "Lou, how long has that hat shop been there?"

"Almost as long as my shop," Lou answered smiling. "The nicest guy runs the place, and you know, he can get quite busy on the weekends, too. I'm always surprised at how many people want those Amish hats. I think there are more tourists that shop there than Amish men!" She chuckled.

Abigail looked at Beth and Beth looked at Abigail. No words needed to be spoken. They were both thinking the same thing.

Chapter 9

"Someone is trying to frame the Amish!" Abigail said in a loud whisper, as they turned onto Main Street. A horse and buggy drove by and they all exchanged smiles and waves.

"I don't know why that surprises you," Beth said. "It's not like that hasn't already happened enough in our own hometown."

Abigail looked down at the sidewalk in front of her. "I know. I was just hoping things would be different here," she said quietly.

Anna reached over and linked her arm in Abigail's. "Wait a minute," she said. "We don't *know* anything."

"*Vell*, we know someone was murdered," Beth said.

Anna rolled her eyes. "*Jah*, we know someone was murdered. But, I'm going to say again, that it is not our job to figure out who the killer is. Why are we so obsessed with solving this crime?" She sounded exasperated.

Abigail stopped and shrugged off her aunt's arm, turning to look at her square in the face. "Because, Aunt Anna, Billingsley is my new home. Those people we met last night? They're my new community. I, for one, didn't meet anyone who I thought could be a killer, and I just refuse to believe the killer was Amish. I guess you could say that I just have a sort of blind faith that it wasn't them." She took a deep breath and grabbed Anna's hand. "I'm not asking you and *Maem* to solve the crime, but I haven't been able to really stop thinking about it since Elise and John first told us about it on the way up here."

"Me either," Beth chimed in. "It's just *baremlich*, and I can't help but want it solved."

"Can we at least try to help?" Abigail said. "Solving crimes is like second nature to the two of you. We may honestly be able to help."

"I don't know how we could help," Anna insisted in a gentle voice, brushing her hand along Abigail's shoulder.

"Well, let's just talk about it as we walk," Beth said, stepping between Abigail and Anna and guiding them gently back on their path towards the inn. "Let's see... what did Elise and John say exactly?"

"*Denki, Maem*," Abigail said, leaning over and giving her a quick kiss on the cheek.

"Okay, fine," Anna said, surrendering her argument. "I think they just told us the husband was murdered and the wife wasn't, right?"

"And they said that the husband was on the town council and that he was pushing a bill to further impose taxes on the Amish," Beth said.

Abigail interjected, "But, remember, Sue at Gladness and Joy said that he was actually really nice."

"*Jah*, that was interesting," Beth said.

"And she said that he and his wife didn't get along very well," Anna said, looking over at her sister and niece, raising her eyebrows.

"Hmmm, that's right," Beth said, her eyes focused on the sidewalk a few feet in front of them. "So, what else do we know?"

"Just what Rose told us last night," Abigail said. "I can't stop thinking about what she said. She was the one who told us that the wife said that the killer was wearing an Amish hat. But we just saw the hat shop. Anyone can buy one of those hats. That's why I think they're trying to frame someone from the community."

"But, did you see how the men acted last night when Chief Edwards and that officer first showed up?" Beth asked, looking side to side at both Anna and Abigail. "I mean, I don't want to believe that someone Amish could do something like that, but it seemed a bit suspicious to me."

"*Jah*, and unfortunately, I think it looked a bit suspicious to Chief Edwards, too," Anna said.

"*Vell*, I guess they could be hiding something..." Abigail sounded unconvinced.

The ladies turned onto the highway. The Hi-Way Inn sign was just up ahead, the Vacancy sign blinking.

They had fallen quiet, all deep in thought.

"Maybe we should just get some rest. Lizzie said that she would have tea and cookies if we wanted them this afternoon, plus we have the leftover care packages from last night if we want more than that," Anna said, as they approached their rooms.

"*Jah*, that's a good idea. Then we'll head back to Main Street for dinner around five-thirty or six," Beth agreed. She turned to Abigail, "I know we didn't come up with any real answers, *dochder*, but try to relax. Sometimes that's what it takes to solve a crime, to put it away for a little while and..."

Anna interrupted, "And sometimes you simply don't have enough information to solve it. You know, it's possible that we will be leaving tomorrow, and then Chief Edwards will have to be the one to solve the crime." She pushed the door to the room open and turned back to Abigail. "Unwind a bit. We've had a really *wunderbaar* trip so far. We've met some nice people, we got to see your beautiful house, and we even found a gift store that will sell your crochet."

"*Jah*, that's very true, Aunt Anna. It has been really great. *Denki* for reminding me of all the good things." She unlocked her door and Angel ran inside to drink water from her bowl. "I'll see you ladies in a little bit."

Abigail watched as Anna and Beth filed into their room, and she followed suit, closing the door behind her. She slumped into the armchair by the bed, looking across the room and out the window at the beautiful trees and clear blue sky.

Angel came over and laid her head in Abigail's lap. "What a sweet angel you've been," Abigail said, as she rubbed Angel's golden fur behind her ears. Angel closed her eyes, enjoying the massage, and rested her bottom on the floor. She lifted one of her front paws and put it next to her face, leaning in closer. Abigail smiled and rested her head back against the back of the chair.

Maybe Aunt Anna is right. I can't let this consume me. I have way too much to think about with the move. Her thoughts shifted to her to-do list of moving tasks. She slid her feet out of her shoes and propped her feet on the armchair's matching footstool pushed a few inches in front of her.

Abigail has just started to doze off when Angel woke her with a quiet whimper at the door. Abigail rubbed her eyes and adjusted her *kapp*. "What is it girl? Do you have to go potty?" She sighed, and slowly slipped her shoes back onto her feet before standing up and stretching tall. "Well, I guess, it wouldn't hurt to go for a short stroll," she said, still talking to Angel. "Let's go see if Lizzie has some tea, what do you say?" She asked, grabbing her shawl and attaching Angel's leash to her collar. She hadn't even emptied her pockets when she came in, so she just grabbed the room key and headed outside.

Angel pulled to the left, away from the direction of the office, and Abigail figured she probably remembered that spot she found earlier that morning and let her lead the way. As Angel found her favorite spot and decided she would once again do her business there after much sniffing around, angry loud voices suddenly drifted their way. Angel and Abigail stood still and looked around. Abigail started to head back, but Angel was sitting firm, looking away.

"Is there something you need to tell me, Brody?" Abigail could only guess that the shrill voice belonged to Lizzie. She sounded as if she had been crying, and Abigail instantly remembered how she had looked upset the day before, when they had first arrived.

"C'mon, Angel," Abigail said, in a low voice with gritted teeth. She did not want Lizzie and Brody to see her and think she was eavesdropping. Angel slowly started to follow Abigail as she walked on the tip of her toes, hoping not to be seen.

"ME?" Brody yelled. "Isn't that interesting that you think I have something to hide?" he snapped.

"Yes," Lizzie said, through tears. "Why is there an Amish hat hidden in the storage room behind the paper towels?"

Abigail stopped dead in her tracks.

"And where were you Thursday night?" Lizzie continued. "You said you were playing poker with the guys, but I know you weren't there. You're lying to me!"

Abigail stood there, leaning against the back wall of the inn, speechless. She knew she shouldn't listen in on other people's conversations, but she couldn't pull herself away.

MARY B. BARBEE

"You are really one to talk about lying," Brody said, his words wrought with fury. "When are you going to admit that you've been having an affair?"

"I'm not doing this with you again, Brody," Lizzie said weakly. "I feel like I don't even know who you are anymore."

"Well, maybe you'd be better off with someone else then, Lizzie," Brody said. "But wait, who would you be with now?" He asked the question with a fake sincerity that was not to be misunderstood.

"Did you kill Jim, Brody? Just tell me you did it." Lizzie words were forced out between sobs.

Brody scoffed. "You know this is your fault, don't you?"

Abigail shivered. She could barely believe what she was hearing, but she was sure that she had heard enough. Her hand reached into her pocket and she felt for the business card that Chief Edwards had given her the night before. She slipped away with Angel at her side and snuck back to her room, locking the door and pulling the curtains closed.

She picked up the phone and dialed the number nine to get an outside line before carefully dialing the number on the card. Her hand was trembling.

A man's voice answered the phone, "Billingsley Police Department."

"Hi, yes, um, I need to speak to Chief Edwards please. Um, please tell her it's Abigail Baker. And, um, it's urgent."

Chief Edwards came on the line just moments later, and Abigail managed to stammer her way through telling her everything she had just overheard. The chief asked her to stay put and keep the doors locked. She told Abigail they would be right there to investigate further and would come to her room when everything was safe.

Abigail agreed, hung up the phone, and wiped tears from her face. She hadn't even realized she had been crying. She stood and knocked lightly on the closed door connecting her room to Beth and Anna's room, pushing it open gently. Angel followed her into the room.

"*Maem*?" she whispered.

Beth was reading a book in the armchair. Anna was sitting on the bed, knitting. They both stopped what they were doing and jumped up out of their seats.

"*Ach du lieva,* what happened?" Beth exclaimed, running over to console her daughter.

Abigail rushed over to lock the door and close their curtains. Then, she collapsed on the chair by the table and told them everything.

After taking it all in, Beth leaned forward and set her hand on Abigail's knee. "*Vell, dochder,* I know that was scary, but I would say that this is *gut* news."

Anna nodded, "And you were right to have faith in your new community."

The three of them peeked out the curtains as they watched the police car park in front of the Hi-Way Inn, and as Brody was placed in the back seat in handcuffs minutes later.

Chapter 10

B eth sat across from Anna at the table, decorating cookies for the upcoming winter festival in Little Valley. Her hands worked effortlessly drawing beautiful snowflakes, or Christmas trees on each perfectly smooth surface, switching up different size decorating brushes every few minutes. Anna was busy wrapping the mini pumpkin bread loaves the two had baked earlier that morning, attaching a little numbered sticker on the bottom of each.

"So, how are you doing now that we are back home and Abigail's moving is right around the corner?" Anna asked her sister.

"I'm doing well, actually," Beth said. "Much better than before the trip." She continued decorating as she spoke.

"You know, going on the trip was really helpful for me. I got to see how quick and easy the trip on the Amish taxi is, for one."

"*Jah*, we are very blessed to have the Amish taxi to travel up to see her," Anna said, writing down how many loaves she wrapped before placing them each carefully in a plastic tub.

"And, of course, it was *gut* to meet the community there," Beth continued.

Anna nodded and agreed.

"I really like Rose," Beth said, smiling.

Anna grinned. "You only liked her because she drives a buggy," she laughed.

Beth giggled, "*Vell*, that's not the *only* reason..."

"I really enjoyed visiting Everything's a Gift and meeting Lou," Anna said.

"*Ach jah*, and I was so happy to secure a place for Abigail's crocheted items so soon."

"And you know we are going to have to visit Gladness and Joy every time we go up there," Anna said, smiling.

"*Jah, jah*, for sure and certain we will do that," Beth said, setting her brush down. She leaned back in her chair and looked at Anna. "*Denki, Schwester,*" she said.

"For what?" Anna asked, leaning back and crossing her arms across her chest.

"*Denki* for being so *wunderbaar* through this whole thing," Beth said. "I know I'm not always easy to be around. Especially these last few weeks, preparing to say goodbye to my sweet *dochder* and the kids."

Anna smiled warmly. "*Schwester*, I wouldn't want it any other way. I am here for you when you need strength, and you do the same for me." She stood and walked over to hug Beth.

Beth sniffled and Anna pulled back, "You're not crying again, are you? I thought you had found peace with all of this," she asked as she hugged her tight again.

"*Nae*, I have. I have. My tears are happy tears. I'm just so grateful for everything," Beth said.

The two sisters moved to the living room. Anna sat in her rocking chair, and Beth sat on the couch.

"Well, what do we do now? Everything is going to be so quiet after Abigail leaves," Beth said.

Anna reached for her knitting and Beth leaned back.

"I'm sure something will come up," Anna said.

"*Ah, jah,* I'm sure. Something always does," Beth said, smiling.

The two sat quietly, listening only to the sound of Anna's knitting needles clicking together. Beth fell deep into thought. She was remembering how just a couple weeks before, she was consumed with worry about Abigail moving away. And she was pondering how the trip to Billingsley changed all of that for her. She realized during those couple of days in that beautiful town that Abigail wasn't actually all that different from her. Beth had faith that her daughter and her family were going to find happiness and success... and, most importantly, that they would be safe.

Maybe it was blind faith, but it was enough.

A town councilman is found dead by the side of Burnt Mill road in Abigail Baker's new town just days before voting on the new bill to raise income and property taxes on the Amish community.

It's true that solving crimes runs strong in Abigail's blood, but she yearns for a quiet life of crochet, morning walks with her sweet golden retriever, and sending handwritten letters to her mother in Little Valley. However, Abigail's new community in Billingsley has very different expectations of her - and they are not shy about asking for her help.

Will Abigail close the loop on the murder so she can get

on with the life she craves? In the first book of *The Abigail Baker Mystery Series*, find out what happens when Abigail decides to set her crochet aside and show the town what life can be like *Where Fear Ends*.

Where Fear Ends is the first book (and the next-to-read!) in The Abigail Baker Mystery Series. Grab your copy at marybbarbee.com!

———◆———

Want to read more about Anna and Beth and their life in Little Valley? Check out all the books in *The Amish Lantern Mystery Series at marybbarbee.com* and get started reading today!

A Note From the Author

Thank you so much for reading *Blind Faith*. It was a great experience building and writing a spinoff to *The Amish Lantern Mystery Series*, and even more fun to write this prequel to the new series!

Readers have asked me why I chose Abigail, Beth's oldest daughter, as the main character in the spinoff series, *The Abigail Baker Mystery Series,* and the truth is that I was originally torn between Abigail and Anna's oldest daughter, Sara. It was only during the writing of *A Blessing in Disguise* when I made my choice. In that book, I had established the town of Billingsley and introduced Angel, Abigail's husband, Jeremiah and their two lovely children, and it just made good sense to me to write more about their next adventure in their new home.

Just as in *The Amish Lantern Mystery Series,* I quickly fell in love with the Amish community in Billingsley, and I thoroughly enjoyed adding a female chief of police, as well!

Although it proved to be a challenge to keep this prequel short, I still had a wonderful time working out all the fun details of the mystery. I hope you enjoyed reading it as much as I enjoyed the creation and writing process!

And now, especially since this is a prequel, I can't wait for you to read what happens next!

The first book in *The Abigail Baker Mystery Series* takes place right after Abigail and her family move to Billingsley, and you'll find that Rose, Chief Edwards, LouAnn and the crew at Gladness & Joy are all waiting for you in another compelling cozy mystery. You can grab a copy of *Where Fear Ends.*

And if you haven't already read the books in *The Amish Lantern Mystery Series*, it's not too late! I have strategically written all of my books so that you can pick up at any point in the series and get started without feeling like you missed something important in the previous book.

Happy Reading!

With so much gratitude,
Mary B. Barbee

P.S. Want to see what I'm working on next? Visit my website at marybbarbee.com

About the Author

Mary B. Barbee is the author of the *Amish Lantern Mystery Series*, the *Abigail Baker Mystery Series, The Pupcake Mystery Series, and more*. As an avid fan of all mystery and suspense in print, on television and in film, Mary B. believes the best mystery is one where the suspect changes throughout the story, keeping the audience guessing. She enjoys providing an exciting escape for a few hours with stories her readers can't put down - and always with a surprise ending.

When not writing, Mary B. is either playing a couple sets of tennis or a strategy board game with her two witty daughters and her kindly competitive mother. The four of them share a home in the Inland Northwest in the beautiful town of Spokane, Washington with their really cute - but sometimes naughty - chihuahua.

Mary loves to hear from her readers. Connect at:
marybbarbee@gmail.com
www.facebook.com/marybbarbee
Instagram @marybbarbee
www.marybbarbee.com

More Books to Read By Mary B. Barbee

THE AMISH LANTERN MYSTERY SERIES
Thick As Thieves – Book 1

Robberies are running rampant in Little Valley, and the quiet small-town lives of the Amish community are suddenly thrown into chaos.

Secrets in Little Valley – Book 2

With the bishop's daughter suddenly missing and a new sheriff in town, Anna and Beth find themselves roped into solving another mystery in their small town.

Saving Grace – Book 3

The Amish community in Little Valley is facing big changes, and big threats, with tourism booming. It becomes clear that some of the new businesses want control of the market, and it looks like they are willing to go to great lengths to get it.

Good Intentions – Book 4

Hazel Thompson is found dead in Little Valley's now-famous Amish Inn, and there's a long list of suspects with plenty of motive.

A Blessing in Disguise – Book 5

Jessica McLean opens shop to find a man has been left for dead on the floor of her diner. Could the crime could be related to Jessica's new relationship with their beloved Matthew Beiler?

Christmas Chaos in Little Valley - Book 6

Beth finds out that the Little Valley library is shutting its doors due to a lack of funding and very disturbing anonymous threats.

<u>THE ABIGAIL BAKER MYSTERY SERIES</u>
Blind Faith – Prequel

Abigail's excitement for her new home is replaced by doom and gloom when she finds out that an unexplained murder has rocked the residents of her new town. And not unusual to her, it's the Amish community that is suspect number one.

Grab your free e-copy of Blind Faith at: marybbarbee.com/blindfaith

Where Fear Ends – Book 1

A town councilman is found dead by the side of the road in the Amish community of Abigail Baker's new hometown.

A Multitude of Sins – Book 2

When secret notes containing serious threats are unveiled, Abigail wonders if the latest victim could have been hiding a multitude of sins.

A Wing and a Prayer – Book 3 ~ COMING SOON!

━━◆◇◆━━

THE PUPCAKE MYSTERY SERIES
Cupcakes and Corruption – Prequel
Battling empty-nest syndrome, Eliza finds solace in the company of her adorable chihuahua, Pupcake, and her dreams of opening a quaint coffee shop. Little does she know that her talent for baking and nurturing also extends to amateur sleuthing.
**Grab your free e-copy of Cupcakes and Corruption at:
marybbarbee.com/pupcakeprequel**

Sweet Suspicion – Book 1
The charming town of Copeland is buzzing with excitement as Eliza and her adorable chihuahua, Pupcake, open their new coffee shop. But when a body is discovered on

the premises, the duo must put down their baking tools and pick up their detective hats.

Confections and Clues – Book 2 – Coming Valentine's Day 2025

Eliza and Pupcake's lakeside getaway takes a dark turn when they stumble upon a body. With a secretive small town and a case no one wants solved, Eliza's sweet retreat quickly turns into another mystery. Can she and Pupcake crack the case before the killer's trail goes cold?

Recipe for Reckoning – Book 3 ~ COMING SOON!

Find excerpts, purchase links and more at
www.marybbarbee.com